I0764356

Currents

Dave Bricker

Currents

By Dave Bricker

Cover and book design by Dave Bricker.

ISBN: 978-0-9843009-5-2

ESSENTIAL ABSURDITIES PRESS

http://www.EssentialAbsurdities.com

CURRENTS IS A FICTIONALIZED ACCOUNT OF ACTUAL EVENTS.

For Ari

There is a tide in the affairs of men
Which taken at the flood, leads on to fortune;
Omitted, all the voyage of their life
Is bound in shallows and in miseries.
—William Shakespeare (Julius Caesar)

Table of Contents

Table of Illustrations

Repo Man

Isleta, Puerto Rico – October 1, 1977

Hanns walked proudly beside *Windship Chaos* as she glided comfortably down twin pairs of rails into the waiting arms of the Caribbean Sea. *We'll have no more unwanted riders now.* Hanns ran his hand across the freshly-dried coat of red antifouling paint on her hull, formulated to put a foul taste in the mouths of friction-causing shipworms, barnacles, oysters and other bottom dwellers who might try to sneak aboard to slow things down.

A half-dozen olive-toned men chattering in Spanish lowered her gently into the water. With a polite bow, one of them gestured for Hanns to step aboard.

What a contrast this was to Rose's boat yard back in Jacksonville where his epic voyage started two years before. Here, everything was handled professionally in a clean and organized facility, a spa for boats that made Rose's look like a junkyard. Built on a small island just off Cabo San Juan on the east coast of the Puerto Rican mainland, Isleta offered a protected harbor with a marina, a comfortable, clear shallow water anchorage and a ferry boat that ran into Playa Sardinera several times a day. A brilliantly engineered railroad system[1] comfortably accommodated wide multihulls like *Windship Chaos,* delivering them gently to a workspace any self-respecting shipwright would be proud to use.

Hanns motored out to the anchorage, happy to be floating again. Even under power he could feel the difference in how *Chaos* glided smoothly through the water, unburdened by the sea growth he had removed with a pressure washer in the yard.

Once anchored in the clear shallows sheltered by Isleta, he traded his boatwork jeans for a pair of light khaki shorts, put on a cotton sun-shirt and, inspired by *Chaos's* renewal, stared into his German blue eyes in the mirror while he shaved the overgrowth off his strong chin. "We're here at the gate now," he said aloud to his ship. "Everything south and east of here defines the boundaries of the Caribbean sea—the *real* Caribbean.[2] Time to start digging into life again."

Tying his blonde hair into a pony tail, he clicked on the radio and gave the output tube a moment to warm up.

"La Vida; Windship Chaos. You out there? *La Vida; Windship Chaos."*

"Chaos; this is La Vida. Whatcha got for me, boy?"

"Forty-foot Hunter called *Robbin' Hood.* Interested?"

1 *Railroad* - Literally a set of railroad tracks that extend from the land down into the water. Boats are floated onto a set of cradles, then winched up the tracks to a work area.

2 *Caribbean* - Though islands from the Bahamas south are often referred to as "the Caribbean," the boundaries of the Caribbean Sea are defined by South America and Mexico to the west; the islands of the Antilles to the east; and Cuba, Jamaica Hispaniola, Puerto Rico, Culebra and the Virgin Islands to the north. Though he's been sailing the *tropics,* Hanns is now poised to enter the "real" Caribbean basin.

"Yeah, man. Good spottin', Hanns. I'm still in Puerta Plata but I'll leave this afternoon 'n' see you soon's the wind'll blow me to ya."

"I had an easy haul-out, Gary. I'm back in the water. If *Robbin' Hood* goes anywhere, my problem will be trying not to get too far ahead of him. I'll let you know where he goes if he moves on."

Three days later, Gary's gaff sails hove into view. Hanns spied his friend up in the ratlines[3] with a pair of binoculars waving back at him. Hanns went out in his dinghy to greet him and carry out his second anchor.

"You ready for some fun?" Gary grinned through his beard.

"Don't you want to get settled in? I don't think *Robbin' Hood* is going anywhere. She hasn't moved for the three days I've been watching. A couple of girls arrived two days ago."

"Nah...when you're huntin' you don't count on your prey hangin' 'round. Anyone cruisin' a stolen boat is gonna be at least a little bit paranoid. I don't want to give him no time to get spooked." Gary put on his cowboy hat, shoved a .45-calibre pistol in his belt and handed Hanns a pump-action shotgun.

"Here's how this works, Hanns. Leave the shotgun in sight layin' 'cross your lap. I don't like to point no guns at nobody 'less I has to. I'll keep the pistol in my belt. We don't need us a confrontation where somebody gets hurt. We'll go up to the boat and be friendly

3 *Ratlines* - rope ladders used to climb up and down a sailboat's rigging

and professional. You just set in the dinghy and smile; you're here to provide superior numbers.

"But I do gotta ask one thing 'fore we jump into action; how you been doin' since your girlfriend moved on? Any fallout? You doin' alright, Hanns?"

"Being alone is hard after sharing so much life and sailing so many miles with her but I haven't heard a word from her or about her. All the same, I'm not going to allow myself to get depressed in a place full of golden sunshine and blue water. I came here to enjoy life; the worst thing I could do is let a misguided stowaway ruin my game. A few months have passed now; I'm over the hard part. I'm sorry about how our breakup went down but the bottom of my boat is clean, hurricane season is over and I'm ready to fly. I'm sure she let the whole thing go; nobody's come along trying to arrest me or kill me, and I'm not hiding from anyone. Life's too good and too short for that.

"My plan is the same as it always was—to make my way south against the trade winds and enjoy the Caribbean."

"Well, you look like you're takin' care of yourself, buddy."

Hanns pinched his recently-shaved chin. "I got a little scruffy for a while but you put things behind you; you get your act together and you move on."

"Well then let's put this work behind us, boss." Gary flashed Hanns another of his mischievous smiles. They motored the inflatable dinghy over to the white sloop[4] and came alongside. Hanns felt a surge of adrenaline; he gripped the shotgun tightly.

"Ahoy, *Robbin' Hood,*" Gary called.

A face appeared. "What can I do for you?"

"You Hanson?"

"Maybe. Maybe not. Who wants to know?"

"My name don't matter. I got a letter here from the First National Credit Corporation of Atlanta, Georgia authorizin' me to repossess your vessel, Mr. Hanson. For security reasons, I need you to read the letter here in the cockpit where I can see you; no offense meant. If you doubt my authority to seize the vessel or the validity of the letter, I have a handheld radio here. We can call the police to settle the matter though I warn you you'll be charged with grand theft if you resist or if the matter ain't resolved in your favor. Otherwise, you got a hour to pack your belongings 'fore I take you ashore."

Hanson sat in the cockpit and hung his head silently.

A pretty face surrounded by a tangle of black curls appeared in the companionway. "Howdy, boys. What's the latest and greatest?"

Gary twisted his mustache. "Sorry ma'am but this boat is stolen property. We got orders to return her to the bank."

Hanson stared vacantly at the cockpit sole. "I'm sorry, Raquel. I'm really sorry. I never meant..."

---

4 A *sloop* is one type of single-masted sailboat.

"Hanson, you're an asshole; the biggest waste of time I ever met in my life. My sister and I dragged our asses all the way down from New York to go sailing because your ad made you sound like you knew what the hell you were doing. All you've done is hit on us since the instant we landed on the dock and now we find out the goddamned boat doesn't even belong to you. Where the hell are we going to go now? I'm gonna sue your…"

Hanns held the dinghy alongside. The sloop's rail came up to his chest. He looked up at Raquel. "Miss?"

"What?"

"I'm Hanns. That trimaran[5] anchored two boats over belongs to me. I'm leaving tomorrow afternoon for a Caribbean cruise; you and your sister would be welcome to come along. She's a big boat and I'd be just as happy not to have to sail her single-handed. No head games—just fun and good company. If you want off, you give the word and I'll detour to the next island with an airport—no questions asked. Why don't you guys hang out with me tonight and make a decision in the morning? No pressure. You took a chance on one boat. Spinning the wheel one more time might pay off."

"You and your sister ain't named on the paper," Gary offered. "You can do whatever you want. I just can't let you stay here on *Robbin' Hood* once the bank officially takes possession of her fifty-seven minutes from now."

5 A *trimaran* is a sailboat with two small hulls or *amas* connected to a larger central hull.

Raquel smiled. "Let me talk to my sister a minute." The black curls disappeared. A few minutes later, two duffel bags jumped through the companionway to the cockpit.

"I'm Raquel and this is my sister Michelle. We'll take our chances with you if you'll take us away from this idiot here."

Gary leaned back in the helmsman's chair mounted behind the stainless steel steering wheel in *Robbin' Hood's* cockpit. "Hanns, I can keep Hanson company for a little while. The man's got himself in a bit of a fix and prob'ly don't need no help feelin' bad about it. I don' think he wants a fight. Why don't you take these ladies back to *Chaos* 'n' let 'em get settled and comfortable? Come get me in a little less than a hour."

Hanns nodded his assent to Gary, placed the girls' two bags on the floor of the dinghy and assisted them off the sloop. "It's a bit of a drop. Try stepping on the engine cover and then down onto the pontoon. Here... Take my hand... You've got it."

The dinghy sped back to the trimaran. Hanns docked its bow between the hulls to make transferring the luggage to *Chaos* and climbing aboard easy.

"Hey, this is classy! I wasn't sure what to expect from..."

Hanns laughed. "From guys who come up to your boat with guns and tell you to get the hell off?"

"Well, yeah."

"This is actually my first gig as a repo man. Gary's the gun nut; the firearms are his. He's something of a cowboy. He can come off a bit rough around the edges, but he's not as eager to pull triggers as he pretends to be and he's a lot smarter and deeper than you might first expect. All the same, when you're confronting people who are about to be evicted from their stolen homes, you never know who you're dealing with. It's just prudent to…"

Raquel shook her curls free of a pink headband. "We're from Israel via Manhattan. A little flying lead is light entertainment to us. We wouldn't be here if we couldn't take care of ourselves." Michelle giggled at her sister's joke.

"Don't worry; I'll make that my job. How'd you wind up on Hanson's boat in the first place?"

Michelle sat down in the cockpit under the canvas and took off her hat. She was taller than her sister, with wavy brown hair, built slightly on the thin side for Hanns's taste. Still, he found the self-assured attitude of both girls attractive. "It was one of those 'friend of a friend of a friend' things," she explained. "Hanson put an ad in a cruising magazine looking for crew. A friend of his recommended it to someone who recommended it to someone who recommended it to us."

"I'm not surprised things didn't work out," added Raquel. "Hanson always seemed nervous and jumpy. He drank too much, smoked in the cabin and made really cheesy sexual innuendo."

"And his idea of cooking was heating up a can of chili!" Michelle added with alarm.

"Oh my God! You do cook real food around here I hope?"

"Rest easy. Good food is fundamental to health, happiness and well-being. We eat fresh seafood, fresh fruits and vegetables and an assortment of dried grains here on *Windship Chaos.* Only rarely will I open a can. I've experienced many times on sailing boats when days of heavy weather will push you to your limits. You can't survive if you're running your body on junk food; it's like running a motor on lousy fuel. If anything, I hope the fare here isn't too healthy for you."

"We may look like a couple of Jewish princesses but I can cook healthy and gourmet at the same time," offered Raquel. "I got hungry enough to eat Hanson's nasty chow last night. I'm ready for a good meal." Michelle made a face.

"Tonight we will dine in style. In fact, if you're game, I'll throw a little party together. I met some colorful folks in the boatyard when I was hauled out. I wouldn't mind seeing them one last time before we go...and a few of them are wonderful musicians."

Raquel raised an imaginary glass to Hanns. "Michelle, we've been here two days and every night there's been some excuse about why the party can't start yet. We've been here on *Chaos* four minutes and things are already hopping. I propose a toast to men of action!"

Michelle raised her own imaginary goblet. "Yes, and to going forward and grabbing some sun in the trampolines[6] up front. They've been calling to me since we first arrived."

"And a toast to good company." Hanns tilted his head back and drained his imaginary glass to its imaginary dregs.

"Can you ladies hold down the fort while I run in and round up the unusual suspects? I'll need to help Gary get Hanson escorted to shore so I may be a few hours. Can I pick up anything for you?"

"I think we're set. Can we do anything to be useful in the meantime?"

"Yes, Raquel; enjoy life while you have the inestimable privilege of living it. There's a good reason they call this moment 'the present.'"

"I think we're going to be good friends."

Hanns stepped down into the dinghy.

"I'll look forward to that…and come to think of it, there is one small thing you can do."

"Sure, what?"

"Please take this silly shotgun and put it down below on my bunk. I suppose firearms have some value when it comes to dealing with certain personality disorders, but they detract from our otherwise festive atmosphere."

---

6 Mesh or fabric *trampolines* are often strung between the bows of multihull sailboats.

The Voyage Begins

THAT EVENING, Gary tied *La Vida* alongside *Windship Chaos.* A number of the dock workers came out in power boats, turning the trimaran and the ketch into a small island of wood, fiberglass, aluminum and revelry. Particularly potent marijuana was passed around, making it delightfully impossible for most of the guests to determine whether the three singing guitar players were actually any good. Not one to surrender mastery of his faculties while in charge of his boat, Hanns moderated his chemical intake and enjoyed a conversation about piloting aircraft with Ramon Remos, a clean-cut gentleman who waved off the joint as it passed by. *"Grácias, pero* I cannot; I work for the government." Hanns was uncomfortable when he found out he had an official on board, but several of his other guests explained Ramon worked as an air-traffic controller in San Juan where he was subject to random drug testing as part of his job.

By ten o'clock in the evening, Michelle felt sluggish, congested and queasy though she had only had a glass of wine. Ramon offered her a room ashore which she accepted, but by morning she was quite miserable, suffering from some sort of tropical flu. Hanns and Raquel were hesitant to see her leave *Chaos* so shortly after her arrival but agreed diseases were best kept off the boat.

They waited in the anchorage at Isleta for a few days while she slowly recovered, ultimately deciding reluctantly that Michelle should fly home while Raquel continued south with Hanns.

In the meantime, Hanns had time to become familiar with his new shipmate. They enjoyed a few daysails. Hanns took her snorkeling on the local reefs.

Raquel was lightly built but what she lacked in physical stature, she more than made up for in attitude. She asked questions, offered suggestions and put her cards unabashedly on the table. "Don't worry, honey; I'm not shy. If I got a problem, you'll know about it. If I'm pissed off, I won't sit in a corner and pout. I'll get in your face and tell you. I hope you'll be the same with me."

Hanns found the openness and honesty refreshing. Being confined on a boat with someone who can't communicate is always uncomfortable. Raquel seemed incapable of restraining herself from doing so to a point some might consider tactless.

"Hanns, my dear, you've been a complete gentleman for three days; you have put absolutely no pressure at all on me. I'm having a marvelous time but something is missing. I hereby release you from your promise not to hit on me. Matter of fact, I'm taking over your bunk. You want to sleep in it, you gotta go through me."

Hanns laughed.

"I'm sure we'll be able to work something out but I'm recently out of a relationship. I can't promise…"

"I didn't ask for promises. I'm asking you to enjoy life like you asked me to. I want to fool around; let's celebrate our time together. If we fall in love, we fall in love. In six months we'll find out if we've become true friends or not; neither one of us has control over any of that. Need a little variety? I don't care. I'm not here to take over your life; I don't want to marry you. I'm having fun. Let's go cruising together and experience life in the islands."

"I just didn't want you to think…"

"I'm a big girl. I appreciate the sensitivity. You're a good guy. Be straight with me and treat me with respect; I don't need to put a tracking collar on you. So far, I like you; that's all I know. I'm laughing, learning and enjoying life's adventure. Let's put a little icing on this cake. The rest can happen or not."

"But where are we going to get six months to find out if we'll become friends?" asked Hanns. "Don't you have to go back to…?"

"My sister and I own a mail order business in New York. The initial work of getting it set up and going has all been done. At this point, running the show is mostly a matter of having the printer send out catalogs every quarter. The fulfillment house makes sure the paper towel racks, coffee cups and crazy straws get sent off to the people who order them. We're not getting rich but the business more or less runs itself. Michelle can manage things quite easily on her own and if I'm cruising, I won't need much money. I'm here. I'm having a good time. I'm thinking I want to do this for a while.

"So when are we heading out, Hanns? I'm ready."

"Next stop; St. Thomas, Virgin Islands. We can leave now if you want. The boat's ready."

"I'm in, boss. Let's go."

"Are you up to learning something about how we find our way around Planet Ocean?"

"Navigating is mysterious and intimidating to me but I guess it's a skill worth having. Let's do this; I'm a fast learner."

Hanns pulled out a chart of the east coast of Puerto Rico.

"In these latitudes we don't get many cold fronts to push us south, though we might be lucky and get a light northeaster. The trade winds are fairly constant all year round. They blow about twenty knots from the east; that's enough wind to raise a pretty good swell. We're at a disadvantage as our destination will be pretty much dead upwind of us until we can get farther east. Once we turn right, the wind will be abeam; sailing south through the islands will be much easier. *Windship Chaos* is faster than most but we can't make any speed until we're about sixty degrees off the wind.

"Think of this as a strategy game. Whenever we can put an island between us and the wind, the seas will be calmer. Close to the bigger islands, you can get some working breeze off the mountains at night but we'll get less and less of that now that we're east of Hispaniola and Puerto Rico; most of the islands ahead of us are pretty small. We'll do a certain amount of island hopping and a certain amount of zigzagging. On an upwind trip, the trick is not to turn the voyage into an Everest expedition; it's not a quest. We may stay in port for a two or three weeks while we wait for the right weather, or settle in somewhere to rest and explore.

"I'll warn you ahead of time, we'll encounter some good-sized seas; the Caribbean is known for that. If you get queazy, seasickness is nothing to be ashamed of."

Raquel took Hanns's hand. "I'll take life as it comes. Don't baby me. I want to learn what I'm doing so you can sleep knowing you've got a tough bitch at the helm who can handle the boat."

Hanns laughed and pointed at the chart. "Okay, here's where we are: off Cabo San Juan on the east coast of Puerto Rico. Due east is Culebra and east of that are the Virgins. St. Thomas is about two hundred miles away but we won't be able to sail directly into the wind. We'll head northeast like this for about twelve hours and then we'll tack back south and zigzag east again. If we're lucky, the winds will be a bit north of east but you can never predict what you'll get. The trick, when you've chosen a specific destination, is not to focus on getting there. What we want to do is go out on the ocean, keep ourselves pointed in the right direction, enjoy life and not worry about how far we have to go or how long we've been traveling. Put one foot in front of the other and head up; the top of the mountain has no choice but to come to you."

Hanns started the engine before turning to walk to the foredeck.

Raquel grabbed the wheel. "I was watching you work the throttle and the shifter when we anchored this morning to go snorkeling. Mind if I try driving?"

"Be my guest. I like your spirit. Watch my hand signals; thumb up or down corresponds to throttle speed; I'll point if I need you to steer somewhere and a flat hand moving side-to-side means 'shift into neutral.'"

"Got it, boss"

"I'm going to drag the dinghy on deck before I haul the anchor. Then we're out of here."

Hanns soon had everything stowed. Raquel drove the boat like she'd been cruising for years. A few hours later, the sun set. *Chaos* blazed over the seas on a close reach.[7] Raquel went below and returned with a bottle of wine. I brought this along for a special occasion; I can't put my finger on exactly what the occasion is but blasting across the ocean like this is an absolute rush."

Hanns accepted a glass and took a sip.

Raquel smiled at him. "Just one question…"

---

7. When a vessel points as high into the wind as she can comfortably sail, she is said to be on a *close reach.*

"Sure."

"Before we left, I propositioned you. How are you going to make love to me if we have to keep steering the boat for the next two days?"

"My dear, that's completely covered. Let me finish my wine and I'll show you how Charlie, the steering vane[8], works."

Hanns set up the device and engaged it with the steering wheel. For a few minutes he watched the compass and made minor adjustments to the angle of the wind vane at the top.

The stars came out. The glow of Puerto Rico fell astern in *Chaos's* shimmering wake—a beautiful evening though nobody remained on deck to appreciate it.

8 A *steering vane* is a wind-driven autopilot. A vane at the top is rotated and set to slice into the wind. If the boat veers off course, the wind pushes the vane to one side or the other. Through a geared linkage, the vane causes a paddle dragging in the water to rotate. The rotation causes the paddle to pull off to one side and this pulls lines attached to the steering wheel or tiller, setting the vessel back on course. The vane pops back up, the paddle returns to the center and the vessel is ready for the next course correction.

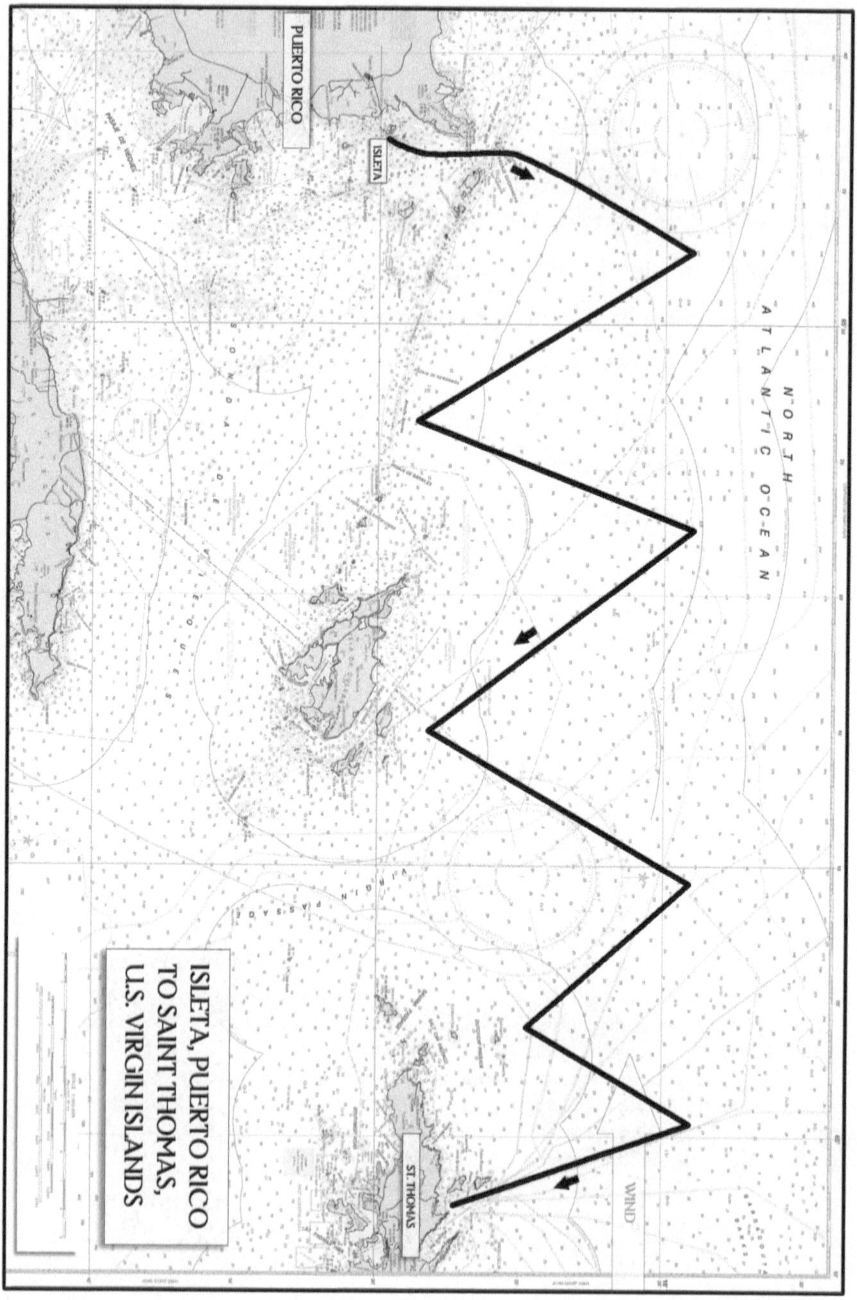

ISLETA, PUERTO RICO TO SAINT THOMAS, U.S. VIRGIN ISLANDS

PUERTO RICO

ISLETA

NORTH ATLANTIC OCEAN

WIND

ST. THOMAS

Becalmed

January, 1978–Three Months later

SOMEWHERE between Barbuda[9] and Antigua, the wind began to fall light. Hanns flew more and larger sails. *Windship Chaos* charged southward beneath a festival of ballooning canvas.

"What's that up ahead of us," asked Raquel, pointing to an unusual, unidentifiable shape on the horizon.

"I'm not sure. I've been watching and wondering; it appears to be a strange ship. We're slowly gaining on it though, so we're going to find out. Ask Veronique to come up and take a look, too."

Veronique, a young Belgian woman, had hitched a ride with them a few days before in Barbuda. Pretty in a plain sort of way, she sported an unkempt mop of mousy blonde hair overgrown somewhat from the neglects of a gypsy life. Though she'd been traveling for over two years, she was fascinated by every detail of the boat and the islands. She proffered questions about things that had obvious answers, revealing an unusual set of perspectives and priorities. Hanns hadn't known quite how to respond when she asked why the sails were white. Jokes flew high over her head but she had a way of

9 see chart page 44

finding joyful amusement in details most other people would miss. She wasn't stupid, Hanns decided, just 'tuned to a different station.' Veronique had little concept of the passage of time and never grew bored. When she offered to work for her bunk by putting a coat of varnish on the cockpit rail, she happily sanded and sang to herself for five hours, lost in the details of her work, clearly unconcerned about putting the task behind her. Hanns and Raquel found her innocence and naivete amusing but they took her aboard as much to protect her from her own vulnerability; she was quick to offer her trust to strangers and they were glad she'd met them before she jumped on a boat with someone of questionable motives.

Hanns adjusted course a few degrees, aiming toward the subject of their curiosity until the strange structure perched atop a hazy horizon revealed itself to be a traditional, tall sailing ship.

"Here's something you're not likely to see. If the trade winds were doing their usual thing, there's no way we could catch a ship like that; she must have a hundred-foot waterline and that makes her fast, but in this light air, the advantage is ours. Let's get closer.

Veronique joined them in the cockpit. She watched quietly as the vessel grew near.

Within an hour, *Chaos* was sailing alongside a three-masted gaff schooner. Raquel took the helm. Hanns stood on the cabin top taking photographs. The *Pernik* had a white-planked hull with traditional black bulwarks[10] over which waved the top halves of about a dozen of her occupants, some of whom pointed their own cameras at *Chaos.* A bare-chested woman in decoratively embroidered blue jeans ascended the ratlines into the rigging to wave at them from on high, her shadow waving in unison upon the wall of canvas behind her.[11]

"A bunch of hippies put together a floating commune over there," observed Hanns.

"People from a disappearing tribe sailing a boat of a disappearing species" returned Raquel. "I wouldn't trade what we're doing for that, but cruising around on a tall ship with a crew of free-spirited people couldn't be such a bad way to travel the world."

Hanns snapped another photo. "The party never stops."

As the wind continued to die, *Chaos* gradually gained more advantage and was now able to literally sail in circles around the larger vessel. Hanns took the opportunity to shoot photographs of her from every angle until the breeze gave out altogether. The seas flattened, forcing Hanns to start the engine and furl his canvas.

Aboard the *Pernik,* the crew lowered and tied down gigantic gaff sails. "Ahoy *Windship Chaos,*" came a voice from her rail. "Come tie alongside. Join us."

10 *Bullwarks* are wooden railings extending above the deck line.

11 *Gaff* sails have a boom or spar (called a gaff) along the top edge as well as along the bottom. A *schooner* is a type of sailing vessel with two or more masts, the largest of which is aft of the vessel's center of effort.

Hanns obliged, placing inflatable fenders along the outside of the port ama to keep his hull from beating against that of the larger ship before motoring over to toss lines to the waiting hands of his hosts.

A man stepped to the rail and spoke with a stern voice. "I'm Captain Norman. Look around but please don't fuck with anything here. I'm running a goddamned ship and…"

"Don't mind 'Stormin' Norman,'" interrupted a smiling young woman. "He's just practicing his people skills."

Norman sneered and walked off as if he had more important business to attend to on a drifting ship on a windless afternoon.

"I'm Bett and this is the *Pernik,* a hundred-and-twenty-three feet of 1920s Baltic trader salvaged from a ship graveyard in Sweden by a bunch of weekend sailors who had a thing for tall ships. They patched her up, and crew members have come and gone over the years. They sold shares in her so the folks aboard now are mostly owner-partners. We're heading down to Martinique to do some work on her."

"I imagine there's plenty of that to be done," noted Hanns. "A ship like this must…"

"You can't possibly know…but we have a lot of fun, too," laughed Bett. "The *Pernik* has enough crew aboard to handle the heavy lifting. Some of us enjoy sailing the boat; others are completely green. Sailing experience isn't a requirement but I like getting involved with working the boat. When things get rough, I feel more like I can do something constructive instead of lying in my bunk and praying we survive."

In company with a few of the *Pernik's* residents, Hanns, Raquel and Veronique followed Bett around the ship as she showed them the galley and a former cargo hold converted into a not-very-private communal sleeping space. "This isn't the *Queen Mary,*" Bett explained. "You get a bunk and a locker; that's your stateroom. There's no vanity allowed. We shower on deck; the head hangs over the stern rail. You don't get room service or maid service but this boat's been cruising the globe on a shoestring budget for years. Some of us have been aboard for a long time. Life's an adventure."

After inspecting the ship, they met the rest of the *Pernik's* crew and passengers. Hanns offered tours of *Windship Chaos* for those interested in seeing her or just wanting a change of scenery. The windless afternoon grew hot. Sixteen naked people jumped from the *Pernik's* rigging into the placid sea to play hide-and-seek between *Chaos's* hulls. Guitars, a harmonica and set of conga drums made their way topside from below-decks. A bottle of Jamaican rum and a joint were passed around, blending the sounds and smells and colors and personalities of life aboard the traditional wooden ship into a pleasant tapestry of song and laughter.

A good-sized black and beige pig wandered around the deck, mooching scraps and greeting people affectionately like an oversized dog. "Don't mind Scallywag," explained Bett. "Norman picked her up back in New England thinking she'd be a good source of protein once we got south. By the time we hit the Caribbean, everyone had bonded with her. She's our friend and mascot. Even Norman has a soft spot for her. We just couldn't kill the pig."

Veronique laughed aloud with obvious disbelief. "You couldn't kill zee peeg?"

"We couldn't," replied Bett. "She's part of our family."

"You couldn't kill zee peeg?"

Bett nodded and chuckled as Veronique repeated her question, trying to insert the concept into her picture of reality like an odd puzzle piece.

"You couldn't kill zee peeg?"

Norman stepped in with his usual tactlessness. "Jesus bitch, what's your problem? We couldn't kill the goddamned pig. What's so fucking difficult to understand about not being able to kill something. Didn't you ever have a pet when you were growing up?"

Veronique sat frozen on the deck, paralyzed, trying not to cry, at an utter loss over to how to respond to the unexpected barb. She muttered an almost inaudible "thank you" to the rest of the *Pernik's* crew, rose to her feet, climbed over the rail and returned to *Windship Chaos* where she went below to hide in her bunk.

"You're a goddamned peach, Norm," scolded Bett.

Norman shrugged and rolled his eyes but the music and other intoxicants soon restored the festive atmosphere. Raquel retreated below-decks with a woman with whom, it turned out, she shared a mutual friend in New York. On deck, Hanns swapped cruising stories with some of the more experienced crew members while relative newcomers to sailing and the *Pernik* listened on.

He sniffed the air and stood up, looking out over the sea. "I think I felt a puff of wind."

"Alright folks, party's over," shouted Norman. "Let's get some sails up and get this tub under weigh[12] again. Hanns, if you're going to hang out here, you'll want to put your boat on a tow line behind us so she doesn't get the shit beaten out of her."

Swimmers clambered up boarding ladders. Crew members donned jeans and shoes and hauled huge walls of canvas aloft. "I've got your boat, Hanns," offered one of the *Pernik's* crew. Hanns nodded. The man untied *Chaos* from alongside, let her drift back and fastened her bow line to a cleat on the aft deck.

The *Pernik* gathered speed, heeling a few degrees. *Chaos* skipped along behind on her towline as the trade winds freshened.

---

12 Though common usage is to say "under way," old ships used a human-powered windlass to raise heavy anchors off the bottom. When the order was given to "weigh anchor," the crew would feel the weight of massive anchors suspended on heavy chains on their shoulders. Once the anchors were aboard, the vessel was considered to be "under weigh." Today, a vessel is said to be making "way" through the water, but this is likely a coincidental evolution based on the homonymous relationship between "weigh" and "way."

Hanns wondered how he was going to get back to his ship. The towline was under great tension; pulling *Chaos* closer was not an option. He considered the relative risks and merits of using the towline as a bridge. The *Pernik* was still traveling at a moderate speed, but if he fell off, he'd have to avoid getting run over. The odds of successfully getting aboard as she went by would be slim.

He abandoned that idea altogether when the tow line slipped off its cleat, leaving *Chaos* adrift, spinning in the *Pernik's* wake.

The Rescue

"*Veronique! Veronique! On deck!*" Hanns called from the *Pernik's* rail as *Windship Chaos* fell behind. "Start the engine. Hold the red preheat button down for five seconds and then turn the key. *Quick!*"

Veronique appeared in the cockpit and looked around helplessly. Hanns glanced forward where Norman held the ship's wheel steady, and smiled to himself. "You bastard. You're not even going to slow down?"

"Got a ship to run. No time for your bullshit," replied the captain with smug disinterest.

Hanns considered knocking him down and taking over the helm himself but he didn't know how the crew of the *Pernik* would react.

Hanns looked back at his disappearing boat, took note of the still-freshening wind and jumped over the stern rail.

Aboard *Windship Chaos,* Veronique succeeded in figuring out that the red button and the ignition key had something to do with making the diesel start. She motored toward Hanns, lowered a boarding ladder and put the engine in neutral when she got close to where he swam frantically toward her. Flustered as he was himself, Hanns was surprised at Veronique's ability to perform under pressure.

Engaging the electronic autopilot to follow the *Pernik,* he gave the engine as much throttle as he dared and began hoisting sails. Each gave *Chaos* an additional boost of power until she was reaching south at a reckless velocity, overpowered and almost flying her windward hull clear of the sea.

"Vat vill ve do about Raquel?" asked Veronique, who for all her concerns about their stranded crew member, seemed unaffected by the frantic speed and turbulence of *Chaos's* race to catch the *Pernik.*

"If we don't overtake her before the wind fills in all the way, Raquel will be stuck aboard until they get to Martinique; they'll get to Fort de France a day ahead of us. Once the trade winds are blowing full blast, we can't keep up with a 123-foot ship."

Having raised and set the sails, Hanns disengaged the autopilot and took over the helm himself. The pressure on the wheel was enormous with so much extra canvas up; he didn't want to break the valuable and important steering machine. For over an hour *Chaos* leaped and crashed, reaching along at top speed in the wake of the *Pernik.* But the trade winds had returned; the gap between the two vessels was widening.

"Can you call zem on zee radio?" asked Veronique, trying to be helpful.

"They don't have a radio. They don't have electric lights. They have an engine they never use. I wouldn't be surprised if they load firewood into their stove. Some sort of 'traditional sailing ship' religious fundamentalism thing is happening on the *Pernik* that defies all reason. The most advanced piece of technology on board is the ship's compass. Hell, Captain Ahab himself is at the helm.

"I'm not loaded with creature comforts on *Chaos*. Other boats are equipped with refrigeration and air conditioning and all sorts of electronic shit that's frankly just waiting to break down. By some standards, things are fairly Spartan here but new tools and materials make sailing a lot safer and more efficient than in the days of the old ships—fiberglass, marine plywood, electronic navigation, generators, wire rigging, plastics, nylon rope, stainless steel, aluminum masts and spars—things the Vikings or early South Pacific islanders would have killed for.

"Tradition is a wonderful thing to build on but people forget: every tradition was once a controversial, unpopular innovation until someone pushed it past the formidable barrier of human skepticism. When you get stuck...." Hanns looked at Veronique smiling blissfully at the sea and discontinued his rant. "How in hell are we going to get Raquel off that damned ship?"

The *Pernik* was at least a half-mile ahead. Daylight was beginning to fade. Hanns might easily have missed seeing a small, nondescript *something* fly off her stern.

"Did you catch that, Vero?"

"Yes; zey throw somethееng over zee side."

"You don't think...?" Hanns handed Veronique a pair of

binoculars. "Get on deck and don't take your eyes off that spot. Forget about the *Pernik;* she's left us behind, but if they just threw in the water what I *think* they threw in the water, we don't want to sail past her."

Hanns reengaged the autopilot, spilled some wind from the oversized jib and ran a smaller sail up behind it before taking down the first one. If Raquel was in the water, blasting past her at top speed would be dangerous.

"Hanns; Raquel ees in zee water. She ees waving at us!"

"Keep your eyes on her. I have an idea."

From a cockpit locker, Hanns extracted a pile of folded nylon mesh—a sea anchor.[13] He fastened the bundle to the aft deck cleats and tossed it overboard. The immense drag slowed *Chaos's* progress to a crawl. Next, he tied four life preservers to four pieces of line and let them stream behind the boat.

"Hanns; over here!" shouted Raquel as they grew closer.

"We're coming. I'm going to sail right over you," Hanns called. "Just grab the ropes on the other side. I'll explain as soon as you're back on board."

Though the wind was powerful and the waves were up, the sea anchor allowed the pickup to happen at an almost manageable speed. Raquel drifted through one of the tunnels between *Chaos's*

13 A *sea anchor* is a large, mesh "parachute" that can be deployed from the bow of a boat in extreme storm conditions far from shore where the vessel has room to drift. The wind blows the boat away from the anchor, keeping the bow of the boat pointed into the seas.

hulls, grabbed the line in the water and hung on tight as Hanns and Veronique pulled her up on deck.

Raquel was beside herself. "That asshole Norman is a whack job! He kept telling me if you couldn't catch up, he'd toss me off the boat; no stowaways or hitchhikers allowed on his ship or some shit like that. I was watching you over the rail and the bastard came up behind me…the next thing I knew I was treading water and…oh, Hanns, I can't believe…I'm so glad you found me…I could have…"

He held Raquel for a moment on the aft deck while she processed what she'd been through, then pulled the trip line on the sea anchor and wrestled it on board. "Veronique, hop back up on deck with the binoculars where you can be seen and keep your eye on the *Pernik.* Raquel, I want you to lie low. Sneak up to the cockpit and sit on the starboard side behind the jib. Towels are waiting for you next to the companionway. I'll explain the aircraft carrier landing after I get this sea anchor up."

Dry clothes and a cup of hot tea soon had Raquel in better spirits. She'd been in the water less than fifteen minutes but the possibility she might not get seen or rescued made the ordeal terrifying. Veronique remained on deck, dutifully surveying the wake of the ship growing ever-smaller before them.

"Norman's a piece of work," explained Hanns, "and while most of the people aboard the *Pernik* seem like decent enough folks, as far as I'm concerned, they're all guilty of sailing away from someone who went overboard. I'm so pissed off I can't think straight. But I felt tension between Norman and the crew; I suspect they're all freaking out over how he dumped you in the drink. I'm sure they've been watching us—hopefully with binoculars if they have anything that high-tech aboard—to see if we stopped to pick you up. Instead of taking sails down, rounding into the wind or making any obvious sign of stopping. I used the sea anchor to slow us down so we wouldn't pull your arms out of their sockets when you grabbed the line. Our sails hid what happened behind us. They saw me switch jibs but as far as anyone knows, that means I gave up the chase. The *Pernik* has absolutely no way of knowing if I picked you up or even knew you were in the water. Vero's still on deck pretending to scan the horizon. If they can still see us, they can still see her."

"But how are we going to deal with this? He could have killed me. We can't just let him sail away and..."

"I know, but filing a report with some sort of rinkydink island legal authority makes no sense. They don't want to deal with the problems of white foreigners who travel around on sailing yachts while they live in one-room houses with corrugated metal roofs. We're in the right but I'm not so idiotic to think some third-world legal system will provide justice and fairness. I'll deal with this in my own way without getting tangled up in it.

"Veronique, come on back to the cockpit. It's almost dark and they're just about over the horizon by now."

Hanns switched on his radio set. *"La Vida, La Vida; Windship Chaos.* You listening?"

A few seconds went by before a burst of static preceded Gary's response. "Hey, *Windship Chaos.* Did you get out of Barbuda?"

"Yes, on our way south now to Dominica. You still in Martinique?"

"Found me two renegade boats down here, but things 'r' complicated. I gotta wait around for some outta-town sonofabitch to come back to one of 'em."

"Well, I'm glad you're there, Gary. I need a small favor."

"Name it, boss."

Hanns explained what happened to Raquel and then continued, "I want you to go down to the boatyard in Martinique to drop off an urgent message for the captain of the *Pernik* before she arrives tomorrow. Write this down for me and leave a note in the office addressed to Captain Norman."

"I'm lookin' right at the office now. Start talkin'."

> WILL BE DELAYED AT LEAST A WEEK MAKING REPAIRS. PLEASE GIVE RAQUEL MY LOVE. FEED HER. GIVE HER A BUNK. I WILL HAPPILY COVER EXPENSES. THANKS AND SORRY FOR INCONVENIENCE.
>
> —HANNS, WINDSHIP CHAOS.

Gary laughed. "Remind me never to mess with you, Hanns."

"No need, Gary. Thanks."

"Any time. *La Vida* out."

"Chaos out." Hanns clicked the radio off.

"I don't get it," said Raquel.

"We could do this formally," Hanns explained, "and wind up stuck for months hassling with some kangaroo court—who knows how it would get resolved or *if* it would get resolved—or we can let Norman and his crew worry about you while they figure out how they're going to tell me they murdered you. If the crew doesn't jump ship or mutiny or turn him in after simmering in a pot of guilt, the morale on board will go a lot farther south than Martinique, especially when they're stuck in a boat yard sanding with the heat and mosquitoes. A chemical reaction is waiting to happen over there; I'm adding a catalyst to set it off. The rest will collapse under the weight of its own stupidity.

"In the meantime we can bypass Martinique, drop Veronique off with her friends in Antigua, enjoy the island for a few days and get on with the business of sailing and enjoying life."

"There ees one theeng I don't understand," said Veronique. "How ees it zey can't kill zee pig but zey can throw zee girl in zee ocean?"

Troubles and Bubbles

February, 1978–2 Weeks later

CHAOS rocketed through the darkness. Raquel ascended the stairs to the cockpit with the Cruising Guide in hand. "I'm excited; they call Dominica 'the nature island of the Caribbean.' The island's all mountains and rain forests, with the world's largest boiling lake in the middle—a volcanic vent. The water is actually boiling; that's not just an expression."

Hanns grabbed the wheel to make a course adjustment. "Sounds like heaven, but we have a little problem to deal with first; the wheel isn't talking to the rudder."

"What do we do about that?"

"Let me get aft to the workshop and check the steering system. The works are under the floorboards."

"I'd offer to steer while you work, but…"

"Lets get *Chaos* pointed downwind. We can drop the mainsail and let the jib pull us. Otherwise this trip is going to become awfully rolly when we drift sideways to the swells."

"But we'll be pointed right at…"

"Right at Guadeloupe? Yes and the Atlantic coasts of these islands are rocky cliffs; they don't offer many friendly landing spots. We're paying the price for sailing on the east side to look at them. In a half hour, we won't have enough sea room left to fall back on Plan B."

"And what's Plan B?"

"Steering with the sails—not a long term plan but the mizzen sail will feather the boat into the wind and the jib will pull her off. If we keep tweaking the sails, we can steer. Way out here, a few degrees course adjustment will point us between Martinique and Dominica. If we get too close to the middle of Guadeloupe, we'll have a lot more land to dodge so let's move quickly."

After adjusting the sails, Hanns removed the quick-release pins holding down the floorboards in the aft cabin and inspected the rudder. "A weld failed. The steering quadrant is attached to a stainless steel pipe that goes up to receive an emergency tiller. Another pipe inside it is welded to the rudder post; the small pipe is turning inside the larger one. The break is two inches above the bottom of the boat—tight working quarters."

"Can you fix the problem?"

"I can't think of another option."

Hanns opened a tool drawer and removed several pairs of locking pliers. "These things have a million wonderful, unanticipated uses. I'll grab the rudder stock at the bottom with one pair and then clamp that one to the floor timber with another to keep the rudder from swinging around."

Next, he unlashed the emergency tiller from under the deck in the workshop, fitted it into the receiving end of the rudder stock and grabbed two small, bronze deck cleats from a locker full of assorted boat hardware. With an electric drill, he quickly installed a cleat on each side of the workshop with stainless steel screws.

"How can you use the electric drill out here away from the dock?"

"A power inverter in the workshop makes 110-volt AC current from the 12-volt batteries. The system's not super-efficient—you can burn through batteries fairly fast if you use a high-powered tool—but for quick jobs, I get the juice I need."

"And the cleats are for...?"

"Watch." Hanns tied a line to one cleat, fastened it tightly around the emergency tiller and cleated the loose end off on the other side. He adjusted each side, tightening the lines as much as he could. "The steering system is locked straight now; the lines hold everything in position. Next, we'll make sure the tiller and the rudder quadrant are aligned properly. I'll drill through the two pipes and put in a stainless steel pin.

"Start the engine," he continued. "Leave it in neutral; I want to keep a strong charge on the batteries. Lock the steering wheel in the middle—a piece of tape marks the center position."

Raquel spun to face the cockpit from where she had been talking down into the aft cabin workshop. She turned the ignition key. The diesel rattled to life.

Hanns lay on the sole[14] in a fetal position, wedged in a small space, his cheek in contact with a beam in front of the rudder post. "The trick will be to bore through all four layers of quarter-inch-thick pipe, and to drill straight and in the center. The job would be a lot easier if the boat wasn't rocking so wildly."

"Hanns, are the trade winds a bit windier than usual today?"

"Yeah...when it rains, it pours. We get an extra ten knots of wind and an extra few feet of swell. Brilliant timing, eh? I thought we'd make better time and get some good scenery on the windward side of the islands. On the Caribbean side we'd have sea room for a week." Hanns tightened a bit into his drill, eyeballed the pipe carefully and began to work as the minutes floated by.

"I see waves breaking on cliffs in the moonlight. How's it coming?"

"Making progress but the steering system has a certain amount of play. On the down side of these waves, the rudder flexes an eighth-inch or so. I have to feel that coming, pull the drill out and put the bit back in when the pressure comes off and the pipes line up again. I'm almost through the first side, though. If we run out of sea room, I'll pin one side; that should be strong enough for us to make it around the island."

14 The *sole* or *cabinsole* is the floor of a boat.

The distance between *Chaos* and the rocky shore continued to diminish. The scream of the drill sounded intermittently as the swells rose and fell beneath them.

"Do you want to take a look at this, Hanns? We're getting kind of close to Guadeloupe."

"No. I'll be through in another five minutes. What time is it?"

"5:30 AM. Should be getting light soon."

"I would love it, God, if once in a while, imminent disaster could visit during daylight hours." Hanns resumed drilling. "I'm through!"

Sitting up, he clamped a piece of stainless steel rod in his bench vice, cut a piece off with a hacksaw and drilled a small hole cross-wise through each end. "Normally, I'd polish the ends. I don't like rough work but under these circumstances, I'll compromise." Hanns tapped the pin through the new hole in the rudder post and inserted cotter pins into the small holes where the pin protruded from either side of the post. "Perfect! Raquel, unlock the steering wheel." Hanns uncleated the lines and gave the tiller a push to one side. *Chaos* responded; the wheel in the cockpit spun a half turn. Hanns removed the emergency tiller and stowed it under the deck beams. "She's all yours. Take us out of here. I'll get the sails adjusted."

Raquel smiled at Hanns. "I think we still have room to pinch[15] around the point and through the cut. Impressive work you did down there, man o' mine."

15 A *pinch* is a very tight reach; the boat sails as high into the wind as possible

To starboard, dark silhouettes of Guadeloupe's mountains rose against the purpling sky, studded sparsely with the lights of houses. To port, the low island of Marie Galante obscured the high peaks of Dominica twenty miles to the south.

Chaos eased around the southern point of Guadeloupe, reaching between the islands into the Caribbean Sea.

After sheeting the sails in tight, Hanns gestured toward shore. "The visible parts of these islands are the tops of an enormous submerged mountain range. The Bahamas are limestone but down here in the Antilles, the islands are volcanic. Dominica has nine live volcanoes; the most active zone on earth.

"The seas are calmer here in the lee of Marie Galante," Raquel replied. "I'm going below to open up some ports and hatches and see about putting breakfast together. Call me when sunrise starts."

Hanns kissed her as she descended the companionway steps.

He sniffed the air. "You got rotten eggs down there? What's the nasty smell?"

"Don't look at me," laughed Raquel. "You're the one who had an extra helping of beans last night."

Hanns smiled. "No; something smells like sulphur." He scrambled back to the aft cabin top, clung to the mizzen mast and surveyed the water. Fifty feet off the port side, a few large bubbles broke the surface. Another bubble rose to starboard followed by a patch of them the size of a tennis court. These bubbles were the size of basketballs, close enough to make an audible *bloop* when they reached the surface.

"Raquel! Raquel! The ocean is starting to boil. We're right in the middle of..."

Hanns gasped for air. "I'm choking. Close the ports and hatches!"

He leaped back to the cockpit to fumble with putting the drop-boards in their grooves and pulled the main hatch closed to seal the companionway. Inside Raquel frantically sealed the ports, unsure what was happening but concerned about the tone of Hanns's panicked voice.

The air in the cockpit became stifling and foul. Hanns coughed and climbed up on the cabin top, hoping to find better-oxygenated air. *Holy shit! We're sinking!* Sea water lapped over the deck, streaming aboard, climbing the cabin sides.

Inside the closed-up cabin, the air remained breathable but Raquel watched terrified as the ocean rose halfway up over the ports.

Breathless, Hanns fell to his knees and clung to the mizzen mast, struggling to stay conscious. His eyes and throat burned.

As suddenly as they had begun, the bubbles stopped. The gas dissipated. *Chaos* rose in the water and continued on her way as if nothing had happened.

Raquel slid the hatch open and peered over the drop boards from the top of the companionway steps. "What the hell was that? Did we almost sink?"

"Almost. For a moment, I think we were sailing through more gas than water. You can sink through a cloud of bubbles almost as easily as you can fall through air. I'm glad the bubble field didn't last too long."

"But where did they come from? What happened?"

"I believe, my dear, we just sailed through a blast of natural gas escaping from an underwater vent; an earth fart."

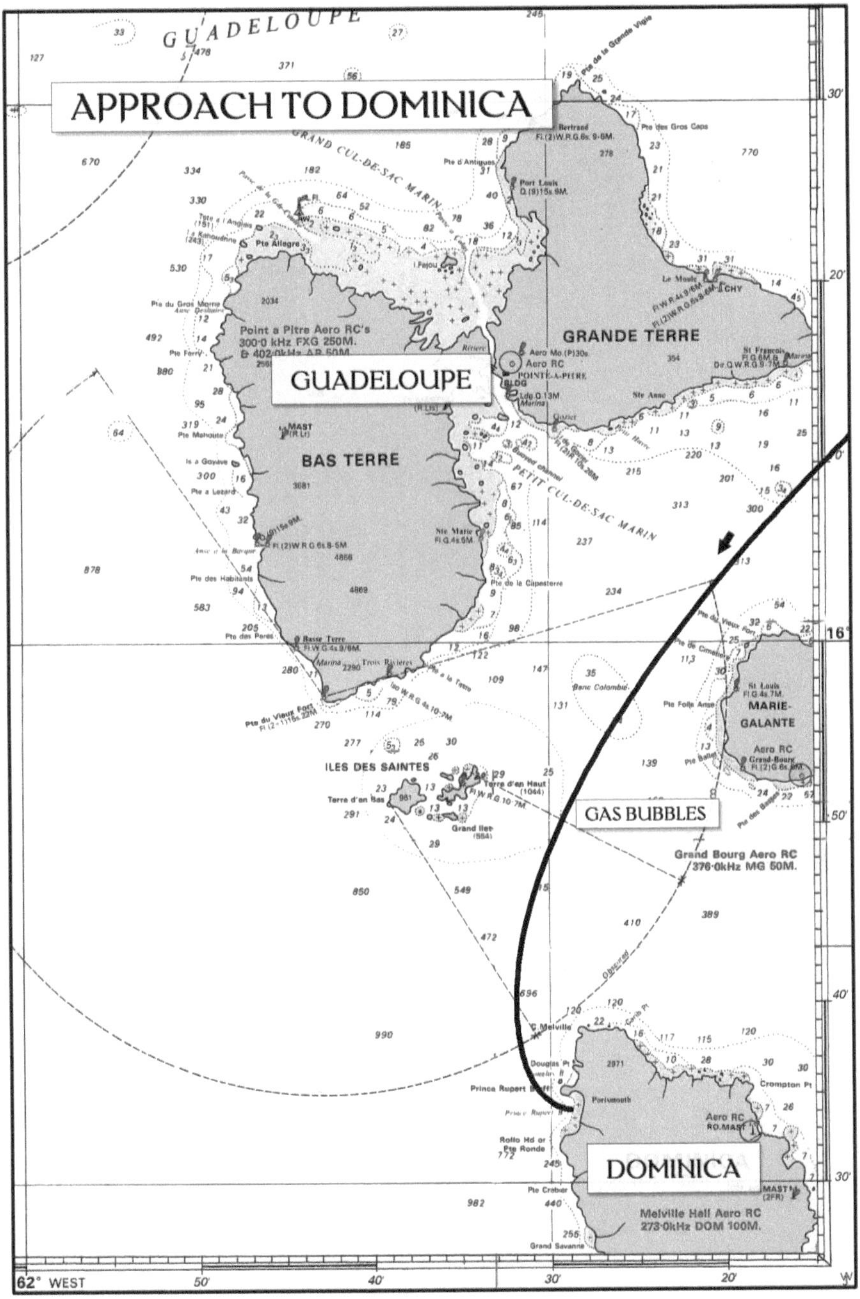
APPROACH TO DOMINICA
GUADELOUPE
GRANDE TERRE
BAS TERRE
MARIE-GALANTE
ILES DES SAINTES
GAS BUBBLES
DOMINICA
Point a Pitre Aero RC's
300·0 kHz FXG 250M.
Grand Bourg Aero RC
376·0kHz MG 50M.
Melville Hall Aero RC
273·0kHz DOM 100M.
62° WEST

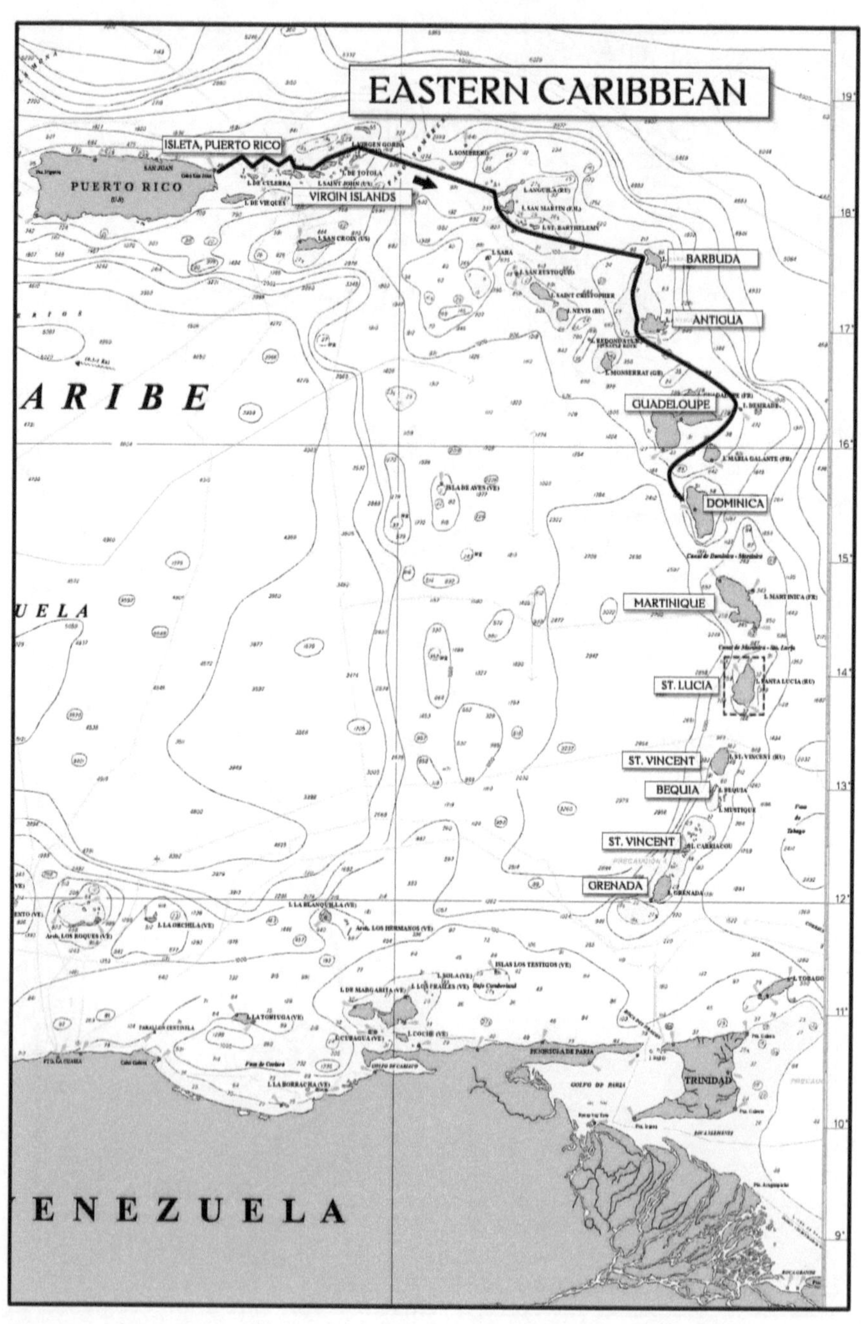
EASTERN CARIBBEAN
ISLETA, PUERTO RICO
PUERTO RICO
VIRGIN ISLANDS
BARBUDA
ANTIGUA
GUADELOUPE
DOMINICA
MARTINIQUE
ST. LUCIA
ST. VINCENT
BEQUIA
ST. VINCENT
GRENADA
TRINIDAD
ARIBE
UELA
VENEZUELA

The Cosmic Lollipop

Roseau, Dominica–February, 1978

Hanns stood at a pay phone at the Cable and Wireless office in Roseau.

"Kalimba, my friend, it's been a while, I know. You're well?"

"Yes, Hanns, doing just grand. Are you still sailing?"

"Uh-huh, but I sold *Sorcery* in K'auai. Now I'm in Dominica on a 47-foot trimaran."

"Ah, I was in the Dominican Republic not long ago. I wish I'd known you were…"

"No…Dominica: pronounced 'dah-min-eek-uh.' The Dominican Republic is on Hispaniola well north of here next to Haiti. I'm down here in a little jungle paradise between Martinique and Guadeloupe."

"Sounds inspiring. I visited Anna and Tino in Ronda a few weeks ago. We were just talking about…"

"Give them my best. I miss you guys, but look…phone calls from the Caribbean to Spain cost a fortune; I'm running out of dimes. I'm hoping you're available for a small job that will give us a chance to catch up in person. You're still flying I assume?"

"You know me Hanns; I fly every day I can."

"Good. I have a friend in Berlin who's a compulsive shopper. If he can get a deal on 1947 Mercedes door handles, he buys them. He owns a warehouse full of some of the most outrageous shit you can imagine. Many years ago he showed me a portable sawmill he purchased at an auction; like a giant chainsaw on a cart. The machine came in two crates: one for a small diesel and another for the cutting mechanism—a beautiful piece of German engineering.

"I'm wondering if you can get ahold of Werner Hermann for me and if you know how to get that piece of equipment out here to the 'middle of somewhere?' He'll be listed under Hermann Industries—shoes, I think. He got the saw for next to nothing and he owes me a favor. He'll be fair. Pay him what he asks; I'll cover you."

"If I can get my hands on the saw," returned Kalimba, "I can probably slip the boxes onto my friend's freight run. He flies through Florida, Nassau, Puerto Rico, Dominican Republic, Martinique and on to Trinidad once a month. He was sick a few months ago and I took the route—which is how I ended up in the Caribbean."

"That would be wonderful, Kalimba. Any chance you can visit? Your wild dreadlocks will fit right in with all the Rastas around these islands."

The voice on the phone laughed. "Well, you know how life goes; the struggle for daily survival gets in the way of so many things we want to do.

"But tell me Hanns, what kind of a scheme do you have going? You're not printing t-shirts or weaving hats out of palm fronds. A portable sawmill?"

"The Dominican Government is selling off hardwood trees way up in the rain forest. They're not deforesting the place by any means but some of the lumber in these jungles is worth a fortune. The problem is nobody can find a way to get the wood down from the mountains to the port. They're up at over 3000 feet of altitude. The rivers are too shallow to float the logs down—and most turn into waterfalls. The terrain is vertical, impenetrable jungle. The roads are way too twisty and curvy to haul anything much longer than ten meters on; driving a jeep up there is dangerous enough. The only reason Dominica wasn't destroyed decades ago by developers is because bulldozers shriek in fear just looking at this place. I'm going to bring in the sawmill, haul it up the mountain and slice the tree trunks up right on-site. I can drag the slices out of the bush one by one, stack them on a light truck and drive them down in as many loads as I need to."

"And what'll you use them for?"

"I'll hit them with a belt sander, slap on some finish and market them as table tops. The grain of these hardwood trees is gorgeous; they'll make beautiful, expensive furniture."

"But where will you store them and sell them? I'm sure the market for that kind of thing in Dom…"

"Still working on the selling part but I'll fill you in when we speak again. Can I call you in a few days?"

"Yeah. Give me two or three days to try to get hold of your friend. I'll look into flights today and try to find a way to sneak a few extra boxes onto the plane after the freight company is finished loading their customers' stuff."

"Will do. Thanks. I hope you'll join me for another adventure."

"Timing's good for me. Talk to you soon. Over and out."

Hanns walked along the Roseau seawall to the Government offices, spoke briefly with a desk clerk and was escorted to a simple wooden door upon which a piece of paper was taped with the hand-written title 'Forestry Minister.' The dark-skinned gentleman inside seemed grateful for some company and something to do.

"Jonathan St. Charles, Forestry Minister. What can I do for you today, sir?"

"I'm Hanns Laldafia. I understand you're selling some hardwood trees up in the mountains?"

St. Charles's face brightened. "Yes, sir. The trees are at the top of the reserve up at Morne Diablotin—some very large gommier trees. If you're serious, I'll take you up to the forest."

"What does 'serious' cost?"

"Fifty dollars per tree but you have to get the logs out without destroying the rest of the jungle—that's the hard part."

"I can afford 'serious.' Let's go."

The road from Roseau wove north along the coast through Mahaut and St. Joseph, patches of Caribbean squalor with corrugated tin-roofed cinderblock houses painted in hues inspired by the landscape. Emaciated dogs lazed in the streets, paying little mind to the wandering chickens. To the east the land rose dramatically. After twenty minutes of driving along the sea, St. Charles turned off onto a street that twisted through groves of mangos and bananas. The temperature dropped quickly as the narrow road gained altitude. Farmers worked fertile volcanic soil on surprisingly steep mountain sides. Papaya, bananas, cacao, callalou and wild coffee blended with natural rain forest foliage. Hanns noted how important it was to honk before driving through the tight, narrow switchbacks. In several places, crumpled remains of rusty automobiles lay at the bottoms of cliffs below the road.

After another half-hour, St. Charles parked the jeep. Hanns followed him up a steep dirt trail, noticing how much easier walking was for his Dominican host who had grown up in this place where flat and level terrain was nonexistent.

They passed a kapok tree with its wide, buttressed roots rising like ribbons of wall, some of them extending from the ground to meet the trunk well above his head. A stream gurgled through a small ravine in their path. St. Charles led him across a fallen tree that served as a bridge. A subtle, woody, organic smell permeated the setting. Hanns closed his eyes and breathed deeply.

"Here's where the trees are." St. Charles gestured with an open hand to an area a few hundred meters in diameter. Four-foot-thick trunks rose into the jungle canopy high above them. A white cloud hovered low over the forest, sprinkling them with rain for a moment before passing on.

St. Charles observed Hanns reaching for his sea jacket zipper and smiled. "Now you know why we call this 'the rain forest.' We get over seven-and-a-half meters a year up here."

"This jungle is beautiful—too beautiful. Isn't it a crime against nature to cut these old trees down?"

"No worries, sir. This is a preserve. Only a few trees will go and only older ones near the ends of their life cycles. When they're gone, the increased sunlight will promote new growth in the lower canopy. We're not interested in chopping down the rain forest—only in thinning out a few areas—and the money from these trees will support forestry and conservation projects."

Hanns walked around the stand, inspecting the trunks, looking up into the green canopy of leaves high above them. He chose two trees that appeared to be situated with the fewest obstacles between them and the trail. St. Charles marked each with a simple piece of yellow tape.

Hanns held out an American $100 bill. St. Charles folded it in half, put the cash in his pocket and shook Hanns's hand. "Thank you, sir. I'll look forward to seeing how you transport them down."

"And I'll look forward to showing you," Hanns replied, "but can I get any paperwork on this? I don't want problems when I show up in Roseau with truckloads of hardwood."

"Of course, sir. Just give them this." St. Charles pulled a pencil and a scrap of paper from his pocket and wrote his name on it.

Hanns stood outside the small cinderblock building with a corrugated steel roof that served as a terminal for Melville Hall on the east coast of Dominica.

"You look perplexed, honey."

"I'm looking at the runway, Raquel. Do you see the windsocks?"

"Yeah."

"The one at this end of the runway is pointing west. The one at the other end of the runway is pointing straight down. I'm glad we're not getting much breeze this morning from any direction. This doesn't look like a fun place to land."

"Well, Hanns. I'm amazed they found a flat, level place anywhere on Dominica big enough to put a runway."

"It's appropriate—nature's way of laughing in the face of anyone who might try to tame her. I love how this island is Mother Nature's stronghold. Anything man builds here will be temporary and insignificant. If you live here, you do so at God's pleasure. If you don't respect the place, you'll eventually fall off a cliff, get caught in a mud slide, catch some sort of tropical fever or wind up with river blindness. In a place like this where you can't beat nature, you have no choice but to join her."

"I'm not used to hearing you talk about God."

"Well, not in the traditional sense but almost everywhere else I've ever been, mankind has dug his foundations and sunk his pilings pretty deep. The land is conquered; flattened plowed, paved and built on. Humans' nests are tough, sophisticated constructions that use miles of wire and millions of gallons of concrete and ships full of chemicals. Some will last for hundreds of years after their inhabitants move on.

"But here in Dominica, man's presence is almost insignificant. If you stop maintaining the roads, they'll be gone in twenty years along with the houses and structures. The jungle and the terrain are so much more powerful than man's tools. Plus, it's a matter of time before one of these volcanoes wakes up and sends all the humans scurrying off. Then, in a hundred years or so—which is a mere instant in geological time—the jungle will grow back and cover the dust as it has for millions of years. Something may be King here but whether or not that something is intelligent or divine, humanity is clearly not in charge—which, ironically, makes the place much more civilized in my opinion."

"Well, sweetie, I lived in Brooklyn for a long time but I grew up near the Sinai desert. The desert is no better place to get lost than the ocean. As much as I love all this nature, I get a rush out of the crazy energy of New York; even from the cars and traffic and noise. The city is a huge, overgrown expression of pure humanity; certainly grotesque in some ways but also overflowing with art and music and theater and culture. Manhattan is a magical blend of comedy and tragedy, adventure and mystery swirling around you."

"That world makes me feel like an anthropologist from another planet, Raquel."

"We're *all* anthropologists from another planet, though not many of us are aware of it. Some people work so hard to fit in; they must actually believe there's something real to fit in *to*, but I love taking a walk in Manhattan and looking at the tall buildings, the bums, the faded posters, the punk rockers and the wackos. *What the hell am I doing here? What is this crazy place? Where do I fit in?* These are all questions worth asking. For me, a ride on the subway reminds me I'll never find answers to them, but at least the trip helps me feel some sympathy for the poor people who think they have.

"Hanns, the whirlpool of humanity keeps me focussed on things that matter. I can't tell you much, specifically, about what actually does matter but I think it's mostly the small, insignificant details; blades of grass growing through the sidewalk are thrown into sharper contrast by the chaos around them. I can't tell you what really means anything but I know it when I see it. The city challenges me not to become numb or callous or hardened. The city makes me laugh. The city makes me cry. The waste, absurdity and unnecessary tragedy make me angry, but Broadway and the music clubs and Carnegie Hall prove every day that the best of humanity's talent, art, expressiveness and spirit are only fueled by the surrounding madness. Impossibly tall buildings show how clever engineers are hard at work advancing the amazing achievements of man to new levels.

"I totally dig being lost in paradise with you, my dear. I can embrace the whole nature vibe and the power of Planet Earth here where volcanoes rise from the bottom of the sea, but don't fall into the trap of believing humanity is all bad. In its most fertile soil, humanity is no more overgrown than the rain forest. There's no such thing as 'overgrown.' It's the nature of things to grow too big or too old or too weak and then collapse, die and regrow. How many times do you think this whole island has been wiped out by volcanic eruptions and how many times do you think the jungle has grown back? Dozens? Hundreds? Thousands?"

"You're right, Raquel. I'm a misanthrope but mankind seems to have evolved to a place where he doesn't know what to do with his primitive survival instincts. He's ruthless, competitive. He's lost his compassion. He doesn't see the forest for the money trees. Aren't you frustrated, living on the fringes of civilization, only to find a thin veneer of human money-economy superimposed where it would otherwise be a simple matter to survive effortlessly in a land of plenty? In more and more places, people want to rent me a mooring and prohibit me from anchoring for free. I pay port charges to step ashore on my own planet. I pay the German government an annual vessel registration fee and I get a worthless sticker in return. Some idiot is always standing on the edge of the volcano doing nothing but extracting fees from anyone who makes the laudable effort to climb up out of the streets to stare into the eye of the earth. I'm amazed nobody pushes the bastard in for trying to turn the world into a peep show. Instead, people passively stand in line and come home with a postcard and a t-shirt. They literally buy this shit and cooperate with these schemes."

Raquel put a hand on her hip. "This is coming from someone who's about to kill two ancient trees in the middle of a rain forest, hack them into slices and haul them 2500 miles in hopes of making some cash. I'm not gonna let you slide. Your nature trip has *way* too much to do with all the stuff you're running away from."

Hanns laughed. "Hey…first, you got me. A part of me is freaking out over the idea of jumping straight from a pristine wilderness into the absolute epicenter of human overgrowth. You're the one with the connections in New York and you're right; there's probably a good market in Manhattan for hardwood table tops. This is definitely a commercial venture but I wouldn't be involved if it wasn't an *ad*-venture. I'm making stories for my memory book here and that counts for something.

"As far as damaging the forest goes, we're not doing any harm. These are old trees. Even if I buy all of them and chop them down, I'm satisfied the Dominican Government isn't deforesting the place. I'm not building a supermarket or a mall; I'm cutting two trees. What gets me jazzed is our venture can only work as a small operation. You could never get heavy equipment up in that jungle for a large-scale logging project. Something like this can only be done by a few people taking a few trees at a time; I'm hardly participating in any kind of 'rape of Mother Nature.'

"Plus, what I'm selling brings a piece of the natural world into the lives of people in an urban environment. Looking at a piece of wood every day is healthy for people. It connects them to..."

Raquel squeezed his hand. "My dear, don't polarize things. In the middle of Manhattan is Central Park. You could get lost in there; it's beautiful. The park is the natural core of the whole City. Central park is loaded with lakes, hills, rocks, trails, meadows, woods and the ancient footprints of Indians who lived there long ago. It's not Dominica but don't think city dwellers are disconnected or they've forgotten about trees and grass.

"And don't forget you're the guy who came up with a shotgun and kicked me and my sister off our boat!"

Hanns laughed.

"You can escape from the human ant hill, but you can't escape being an ant," Raquel continued. "Joke all you want about seceding from the species but that ain't gonna happen. We're evolutionary adolescents. We humans are driven by our ancient animal instincts, inspired by our vast potential to create something powerful and transcendent, enslaved to our higher mammals' unique capacity to seek and experience pleasure, and burdened by our uniquely human search for meaning. Some adolescents don't survive the crazy things they do. Some wind up addicted to unhealthy pleasures. Some get knocked up or knocked down before they grow up. You must have been a hell of a teenager yourself, but the clever ones like us get out of all the amazing and stupid trouble we get ourselves into and wind up a little wiser. The best of us grow into adulthood without losing our childhoods but we all have to find our way, both as individuals and as a young and reckless species.

"Somewhere deep inside us, at the center of all the conflict, I believe there's a little core of truth we spend our lives trying to drill down to. But I think if we could ever actually lick our way down to the middle of the cosmic lollipop, we'd end up disappointed, staring at the empty stick. There'd be nothing left, no flash of light, no sudden realization. Life is all about the sweet journey to the center we're on as individuals and as children who inherited a planet we don't quite have the awareness to care for yet."

"Your perspective is certainly more balanced than mine—and I love you, Raquel—but don't you think *homo sapiens* is destroying this planet? Don't you think a few of us are making life a lot harder for people who could eat better, live better and spend more time enjoying the gift of being here?"

"Absolutely, and our efforts to confront those problems are part of how growth happens. I'm not telling you to sit passively by and meditate. I'm saying the people who fight wars, steal car stereos, smuggle cocaine, charge admission and chop down trees in the jungle are all part of the human dance. We're all teenagers taking the risk of being caught or killed so we can feel powerful, enjoy a thrill or try to make the world a better place for everyone. We'll either survive or we won't. Ultimately, we'll all get left holding the stick. Then we'll look back and see if our lives were sweet. Everything will eventually get wiped out by volcanoes, ice ages, meteorite strikes and the implosion of the sun; the earth will be a big ball of carbon one day. Life is a short movie but we get to act, direct and even write some of the script.

"I'm just reminding you that Dominica and Manhattan are part of the same planet. Designing a cruising boat and designing a skyscraper are both advanced and beautiful forms of human expression. Selling stocks and selling black coral jewelry to power boaters are equally humble, wonderful, terrible and commercial endeavors. We all live in one world; whether *your* world is ugly or beautiful has only to do with your perspective. Don't carve the universe up into good and bad. Drink up and experience all of life's flavors while you're here, even the bitterness."

A small, twin-engine aircraft flew low over the airfield, gained altitude and banked sharply, turning to stab a wing toward the runway and leveling out at the last second. A moment later, the plane taxied up to the front of the terminal and shut down its engines. A side door opened downward. A few dark-skinned people exited using the stairs on the inside of the door.

Hanns and Raquel waited inside a roped-off area for the cargo to be unloaded.

A slightly overweight man wearing a pith helmet and a beige photographers vest studded with empty pockets descended the steps and walked toward them, ignoring the painted lines on the tarmac leading to the customs office. He waved at Hanns before a young lady in a green uniform escorted him back between the yellow lines.

"Well, my dear, things have just gotten a bit more interesting," Hanns chuckled, waving back. "Werner Hermann has come in person. I doubt he's ever taken a walk in the woods. He's a sweet guy—extremely easy-going with a great sense of humor. You'll like him but his major calling in life is to act as the beneficiary of his father's will. He has absolutely no idea what he's gotten himself into. This is going to be interesting."

Raquel smiled at Hanns. "If the city wants to come to the jungle before the jungle goes to the city, the arrangement seems appropriate enough to me."

Business Partners

"HANNS! So good to see you after all these years. Your friend Kalimba told me what you were up to. When he told me he wasn't going to be able to make the trip, I thought what the hell; how can I turn down an adventure on a tropical island and a cruise in the Caribbean? I'm curious about your forestry venture? Do you mind if I ask you about the details? I may be a chubby forty-year-old whose biggest outdoor expedition was a trip to the mailbox in a blizzard but business is something I understand well."

"Yeah...I'd be grateful for any advice you might give. We own two trees about 130 feet high each. If we take our time and set things up right, we'll be able to get two-inch-thick table tops out of them."

Werner pulled a note pad and a pencil from one of his many pockets. "135 feet times two is 270 feet. Multiply by six slices per foot and we get 1620 slices."

"Let's figure 1,500. The saw blade will eat some and parts of the trees, especially near the tops, are mostly branches. We might get some bar stool tops out of the thicker parts of the branches but we won't know until we get the trees down on the ground and start cutting."

"And how much do you figure you can get for each slice?"

"Once they're finished, we can probably get at least $500 each. We'll test the market when we get to New York but I've seen hardwood table tops in high-end furniture stores in Berlin and…"

"Ya, easily. I looked around and called some furniture shops and interior designers before I left. You can probably get more depending on what the wood looks like. A slice of tropical hardwood is quite a bit more dramatic than a slice of pine.

"What will your expenses will be, Hanns?"

"Mostly labor. I need to buy a small flatbed truck and gas. I figure on about two weeks of busting my ass up in the jungle with the saw and a pair of earplugs. I'll need a small freighter but I can hopefully sell the boat afterward for more or less what I pay. Fuel for the trip to New York will cost some money; by my calculations…"

"Why New York? Why not Florida or some place not so far away?"

"Apparently Raquel is in with Manhattan's Jewish Mafia. She…"

"Sweetie, they're not the Mafia." She put her hands on her hips.

Hanns smiled. "No, they're not the Mafia, though the rabbi controls half the city. Anyway, a warehouse is already arranged for us to use at no cost. If they don't excommunicate her when they find out she's shacking up with a kraut, we'll be set up with a place to sand and finish the table tops, store them and sell them. The floor space will cost more than the fuel savings anywhere else."

"Well, I want a piece of the action," proposed Werner. If you'll accept me as a partner, I'll finance the expenses, help with the work and split the profits with you. Either way is fine but I just flew over this place; getting your lumber out of the jungle and down to a ship is going to be one hell of a job."

Hanns paused, squeezed his chin between his thumb and forefinger and looked at Raquel. "Y'know what, sweetie? Let's do this thing in style. I'm not one to shy away from hard work but parts of this operation aren't going to be fun. Slicing the trees is one thing but hauling 1500 heavy table tops through the jungle to a truck won't be easy. The sanding won't be grand entertainment either. Let's hire a few laborers to do the heavy lifting. I'll pick the most talented ones and train them to work with the saw so the slices come out the way we want with minimal waste. We'll find no shortage of adventure up in the rain forest or in hauling this stuff 2,500 miles to New York City; that will be an adventure in itself. I've bootstrapped everything I've done my entire life but if you don't object to parting with half our share, we'll earn plenty of money to go around in exchange for a lot less physical labor."

Raquel smiled. "Under one condition; too many fifty-fifty partnerships wind up in deadlocked control battles. We keep 50.1% and Werner, you get 49.9%. We can tip you the difference if you like but I want Hanns in charge. He's an unbelievable do-it-yourselfer.

You'll probably be the one pushing him to spend money, but when a call needs to be made, I have faith in his planning and intuition. You may be just as brilliant, Werner, but I don't know you well enough to bank on you. By all means, contribute your ideas and expertise, but when we're up in the rain forest or out at sea, I want to be confident my ship has one captain at the helm."

"Raquel, I like you already. Unequal partnerships are smart business and a good recipe for keeping friendships alive. I wouldn't want things any other way. I'm no outdoorsman but I realize a pocket calculator isn't going to be the main decision-making tool out in the bush. All the same, I did do business with a rabbi once. Everything was based on a handshake. The transaction was as honest as you could ever hope for, but a deal is a deal is a deal is a deal. I was glad I spelled out a few terms in advance."

The three shook hands. Hanns went over to speak with one of the airport officials before returning.

"Let's start by picking up a vehicle," suggested Hanns. "I saw one or two for sale and one's not far from the airport. Werner, do you have American dollars?"

"Way ahead of you. I exchanged my *deutschmarks* back in Berlin. I figured American cash would be king in the Caribbean."

"Smart man. Let's get a taxi and see if that truck parked outside of Mahaut is available. Otherwise, I passed one for sale in

Massacre. That one's a bit more beat up but it might do fine for our humble purposes."

"When did you get a chance to look for trucks?" Raquel laughed. "Are you sneaking out at night or something?"

"No. When St. Charles took me up to check out the trees, we drove along the coastal road and back down to Roseau when we were finished. I paid attention because I wanted to be able to find my way again, and I was thinking about how to move the wood down from the jungle on the winding roads. I haven't mentioned this yet, but the crazy idea occurred to me to take some of our profits and possibly buy a piece of land here. We could build a little tree house, plant some fruit trees and put in a garden. You can plant aluminum baseball bats in this volcanic soil and grow full-sized telephone poles in three weeks! Anyway, I started looking at what was advertised for sale on the roadside as far as cars and property, and I took note of a few trucks. They're not pretty but if one will handle the terrain here for a few weeks, I'll be just as happy to buy something ugly and cheap."

Werner smiled at Raquel. "Does his brain ever stop?"

"No, but he has an aptitude for making his wacky ideas come to fruition. The trait can be a little maddening at times because you never know what kind of outrageous impulse is about to spontaneously explode past the imagination stage, but I find it endearing and inspiring. How many people dream this much, accomplish this much and live this much? I wish everyone could live in a world of so much potential. Too many people stop dreaming because they don't think they *can*. Those kinds of limitations never occurred to Hanns. When you're with him for any length of time, your own perspective becomes one of vastly expanded possibilities."

"Other people let their fears and insecurities hold them back," chuckled Hanns. "There's nothing exceptional about me. Plenty of people have brains, talent and education; most of them get distracted by things that don't matter or they're taught to accept imaginary limitations. My personal religion doesn't acknowledge the existence of impossibility and my life runs on that faith. If I can't accomplish what I set out to do, my entire belief system will crumble."

"Personal religion? Werner's been here for ten minutes and I'm already finding out things I never knew about you."

Hanns smiled. "My 'religion' is nothing structured—more a figure of speech, to be honest. My life doesn't revolve around accomplishing tasks. I set out to do things and got my ass kicked plenty of times, but I also survived plenty of situations where, by all odds, I should have been killed. Even when something doesn't work out, I end up learning something or discovering a different direction. Maybe I'm a natural improviser? I take what life gives me and I do something with it. I'm here living with a gorgeous woman on a sailboat anchored next to an exotic island. Now, I'm ready to embark on an adventure that will take me from the rain forest to New York City. I don't know what will happen but I find something validating about being here in this moment with you two on the cusp of this chain of events. I attach no formal worship or theology to anything, but the Universe encourages me. I'm doing something right; I don't care if my sense of validation is internal or external or neither or both. If I start believing in limitations, they'll become real so I keep dreaming and I keep pushing and I keep taking chances and I keep getting away with it all. Life is good and the Universe keeps on laughing with me. That's all there is to it; no rule books or churches or spiritual guides. I live life to the fullest and try not to do it on anyone else's back."

Raquel gave Hanns's hand a squeeze and smiled. "What do you guys want to do, assuming we find a vehicle in the next few hours? Werner, do you want to go out and get settled on *Windship Chaos*?"

Werner locked his hands behind his head, stretched his elbows back and yawned. "Enough sitting around. Let me take us all to town for a nice lunch to start off our partnership and then, let's get this saw up to the jungle and cut down some trees."

Gift Horse

Government Docks, San Juan Puerto Rico – March, 1978

AFTER thanking the taxi driver, Werner, Raquel and Hanns walked down the pier, boarded a rust-streaked ship and descended a creaky metal stairway into the cargo hold. The hum of an electric pump accompanied a watery sound from under the floorboards, many of which were soggy plywood replacements for decks that had long since rusted through. Two flickering yellow lights illuminated a dreary space, though the green steel bulkheads displayed empty receptacles for at least four more bulbs.

Hanns shrugged. "She's not pretty but if she'll stay afloat, she'll do the job. At sixty-five feet, you won't find anything smaller that still qualifies as a bona fide cargo boat. She doesn't draw too much, she's not made of wood and she's small enough to handle like a yacht. We don't need a full-fledged ship on our hands."

"She lists to one side," observed Werner.

"I'm wondering about that, myself. I can't figure out why. Something's got to be off-balance." Hanns smiled. "Maybe the starboard side has lost more metal to rust?"

Turning the wheel lock on the heptangular[16] door to the engine room, Hanns fumbled for a light switch. Finding none, he switched on his flashlight and laughed. "Now *this* is a museum piece; an original one-cylinder diesel; probably about fifty horsepower."

Raquel grabbed his arm. "Do you think she'll run?"

"The wonderful thing about these engines is they don't have many parts to break. If this motor's not frozen—and it appears to be the only part of this boat anyone cared about for the past thirty years—it should run forever." Hanns pulled the oil dipstick and shined his light on it. "See? Pure golden honey."

Werner stared at the machine critically. "I don't know much about engines, but fifty horsepower doesn't seem like a lot."

"You're right, but she's not built for speed; she's built for reliability and torque. She's got a big, low-pitched prop. If she were an automobile, she'd make a terrible race car but she'd make a wonderful tractor. Boats like this were built to shuttle sardines between New England fishing boats and processing plants on shore, probably during the late forties after the war. She's a relic from the early days of factory fishing, back when they first decided the oceans were a resource to mine without limits twenty-four hours a day. She was designed to haul heavy loads in heavy seas. I'm sure her salty cargo contributed to all the rust eating her today. I'm liking the big new

---

16 A *heptangle* is a rounded rectangle.

aluminum fuel tank though. Her previous owners obviously wanted long range and clean diesel."

"But is she safe?"

"She's been floating here at the dock for a year, though I imagine not without the help of a few pumps. She does have an eight man life raft with a recent inspection certificate. That mitigates a certain amount of risk."

"I wonder," said Werner, "how an old boat like this winds up in a government auction in San Juan, Puerto Rico."

"Easy; she's a perfect drug boat. She's got a hull with so many shades of peeling green paint, she's almost camouflaged. Someone installed a big fuel tank for long range and she can hold several tons of cargo. I imagine most of these boats came here the same way; they're all DEA[17] seizures."

"Aren't you worried a doper will outbid us on her?"

"I suspect the drugrunners don't want the government to know when they buy a boat like this; they can buy vessels from plenty of other sources. Most of the bidders will be people looking for deals on speedboats and sport fishermen. Possibly, a few carpenters-speculators might want to put a new interior in a stripped boat so they can resell her. But I haven't seen anyone else climbing all over this one. We'll grab her for nearly nothing and if not, *c'est la vie.*"

---

17 The DEA is the United States Drug Enforcement Agency

"But Hanns, won't you wind up on a government list, yourself?"

"Possibly, but I'm a documented non-smuggler; that's a long story.[18] Also, our cargo will be entirely legit. If they want to waste their time searching me or following me, let them."

Two sparse cabins at the nameless freighter's deck level supported a low-ceilinged galley and dining area on top of which squatted a pilothouse—little more than a bare metal room with windows. A few modern navigation instruments and a VHF radio remained aboard, left by previous owners. Hanns turned the wheel and tried the gear and throttle linkages. "We found an ugly duckling."

Hanns descended the stairs to the deck and hailed a uniformed man on the dock. "Do you know anything about this boat?"

"Si, Señor. I take care o' her this pas' year. She not a look so good, but I starta-de-engine a few weeks ago. She leak; you gotta keep de pump runnin', but she a good little freighter. I put in de 'lectric pump so you no gotta run de diesel pump alla de time. Nobody wan' her; she been here long time. You bid eight thousand dollars, you take her. Eight thousand dollars."

The rusted freighter was the last boat on a list of a few dozen being auctioned off. By the time she came up for bid, the only people left in front of the auctioneer were Werner, Hanns, Raquel and a group of Haitian men. Werner bought the freighter 'as-is, where-is' for $7500.

18 This story previously told in *Waves* by Dave Bricker, 2010

"Two or three months and she's yours," Hanns explained to the disappointed Haitian bidders. "We won't need her after that and she'll be in much better shape when I'm done with her." One of the men scribbled his contact information on the back of his copy of the auction list. Hanns put the note in his pocket.

Hanns handed Raquel a pen. "This one's going in your name."

"Oh, darling. A present? For me? Really, you shouldn't have."

"The politics will go easier if you, a U.S. citizen, buys the boat from the U.S. Government. It'll be a fustercluck to put her under a German flag and then deal with bringing a foreign boat into a U.S. port. You're the owner. You're the Captain. You have an American address, right?"

"Technically, yes, but Michelle put all my stuff in storage. The landlord's an old friend; he'll pass my mail to Michelle but God only knows who's living in my old apartment."

"So much the better—another layer of anonymity and insulation."

"But why do we need that? We're not doing anything illegal."

"Sweetie, anything that separates me from government agencies, lawyers, tax collectors, salesmen and other institutionalized scam artists will only add a measure of simplicity and tranquility as I pursue my peaceful business strategies in the land of the open palm."

Raquel rolled her eyes before leaving to get a second taxi-load of food and supplies. Hanns changed the filters, cleaned out the water separator and bled the fuel system. Two new marine batteries revealed most of the running lights to be in working order, and he installed two 12-volt marine lights in the engine room. He repacked the stuffing box where the propeller shaft exited the hull, which didn't stop the water from entering altogether but slowed the leakage.

Werner explored the ship, poking through lockers and opening hatches. He was more than a little disappointed but did his best not to show it.

An hour later, a clattering of feet reverberated on the steel deck. Hanns ascended the rusty steps. Raquel turned the light on in the galley. A half-dozen cockroaches scattered. "Y'know, Hanns, this isn't exactly luxury cruising. You drag a woman into something like this, you're gonna have to pay."

Hanns laughed. "Don't look a gift horse in the mouth. We stole this baby. Also, you know I'm all for neat and clean myself. A day or two of cleaning and painting will make her much more pleasant to run, if not more buoyant. Did you get the bug bombs?"

"A dozen of them."

"We'll fumigate the cargo hold and the cabins on the way back. Once we're home on *Chaos* in Dominica, we'll bomb the rest of her. Every room on this ship has a watertight door. The people who built this tub probably built ships for the U.S. Navy during World War II. The idea was to keep leaks, damage or fire as isolated from the rest of the ship as possible. Steel doors work for sealing up bugs and rats with the poison, too."

"Rats?"

"Well, I haven't seen any...but forget I said anything. Can I show you something cool?"

"As long as it's not rats, sure."

"Follow me down to the engine room."

With a large lever, Hanns turned the flywheel over slowly a few times to distribute oil through the single cylinder. Then, he gave the lever a strong pull and closed the compression lever on top of the cylinder head. A small explosion was heard and the flywheel began to slowly rotate.

Werner appeared in the engine room doorway. "Is that all? I thought..."

Boom. The flywheel turned slightly faster now.

Boom boom.

"Oh, I..."

Boom boom boom.

Boom boom boom boom.

Hanns motioned for Raquel and Werner to follow him away from the din and closed the door behind them.

"This engine has a super-heavy flywheel. It takes a short while to get going but once that weight is spinning, nothing can stop it. The sound of a single cylinder diesel starting up is delightful. You can run these machines for months at a time; they're the hardiest things on the planet."

"Spoken like a true man," observed Raquel.

"Maybe, but the engine is the saving grace of the whole ship. She has a smaller sister diesel for the main pump, too."

"Does it run?"

"Probably, but if not, we can use the electric one. They're going to start charging us dockage as of tomorrow morning so if the diesel pump won't start, we'll fix it under weigh or when we get back to Dominica."

Hanns flipped on the running lights. Raquel and Werner uncleated the dock lines and followed them aboard before joining Hanns in the pilothouse.

Raquel put a folder full of ship's papers down on the chart table."So what are we going to call her?"

"I got the idea from you, Raquel. What do you think of *Gift Horse*?"

She put an arm around Hann's waist and giggled. "More like Gift *Hearse*!"

Hanns bowed to his crew theatrically. "Four hundred miles to Dominica; we'll be home in two or three days."

"My fingers are crossed," said Werner with lighthearted cynicism. "You're sure the life raft has fewer holes than the ship?"

The dark freighter slipped around the jetty and rattled into the Puerto Rican night.

South Street Pier

May, 1978

Hanns studied the Brooklyn Bridge from the pilothouse. "We'll fit right in here. This whole South Street Pier area doesn't look much better than our rusty old derelict vessel."

"Well, we can't just tie up somewhere and hope nobody notices at 3:00 in the afternoon."

"Werner, half the waterfront is abandoned—falling into the sea. Raquel says they're planing to fix up some of the funky buildings but people have more important things to worry about than why a dilapidated old freighter is tied to a dilapidated old dock…it all kind of freaks me out, actually."

"Ya, how come?"

"I've been living in the islands for almost two years; a few trips to San Juan hardly count for much. I haven't seen a building higher than four stories or any kind of heavy industry for a long time. My 'filters' are gone. This place is buzzing."

"That's what New York City does. How about docking over there?"

"Behind the sunken wreck?"

"Exactly."

"Good eye. Can't say what kind of shape the dock will be in, but let's give her a try. The fuel gauge is on 'D'."

"D?"

"'F' is 'full.' 'E' is 'empty.' We need a lower letter for our situation."

Hanns aimed *Gift Horse* toward the pier. The engine ran rough for a few seconds and died. Hanns cranked the wheel to starboard. The rusty ship bumped lightly against the old wooden dock and came to a gentle stop. A piling disintegrated into a cloud of termites as the ship contacted it. Werner stepped off onto the uncertain pier with a bow line which he secured to one of the few pilings that wasn't about to fall off, then walked aft to catch a stern line from Hanns who ran down to the deck from the pilot house.

"Be careful, Werner. Some of the planks are gone. You definitely don't want to fall into this nasty harbor water."

"Thanks. What are we going to do about the pumps? We're out of fuel for the diesel. I doubt we'll find any electricity on this pier."

Hanns thought for a moment. "You might be surprised. The City probably keeps the lights working to discourage crime—not that that stands much chance of being effective—but I'm hoping we can hijack some juice here. Otherwise, we can run off batteries for a day or two. There's plenty of time to go fill some diesel jugs. The small pump engine only burns a few gallons a day."

Werner stepped back aboard. Hanns followed. "What about customs and clearing in?"

"What about it?"

"Shouldn't we?"

Hanns laughed. "I suppose we probably *should* but if nobody asks any questions, I'd prefer to mind my business and keep a low profile. If anyone does ask, we'll play dumb, speak German and show them our passports. They'll send us off to immigration to fill out forms and pay some sort of extortion fee. Let's skip the international politics and call Raquel."

Hanns followed Werner up the stairs to the bridge. He grabbed the microphone and switched on the VHF radio.

"Marine operator. Marine operator. This is *Gift*...er...excuse me...*Windship Chaos.* I'd like to make a call, please."

"*Windship Chaos,* New York City marine operator. Stand by please."

"*Windship Chaos* standing by."

A few moments went by before the operator returned. *Windship Chaos,* what name and number please?

"This is Hanns calling for Raquel at 212-312-0700."

Stand by, *Windship Chaos.*

Hanns heard the ringing. Michelle answered, accepted the call and passed the phone to Raquel.

"Go ahead *Windship Chaos.*"

"Honey, I'm home."

"Where have you been? You're late. Have you been drinking again?"

They both laughed.

"We're tied up where you said, just outside the Brooklyn Bridge. The dock's pretty rugged but the price is right."

"I'll be down in about twenty minutes. I'm not far away."

"Looking forward to it. I love you."

"Love you, too."

"Thanks operator. No further calls."

"Thank you *Windship Chaos.* Marine Operator out."

"*Windship Chaos* out."

Werner put on a pair of slacks, a button-up shirt and a sweater vest and returned to the bridge.

"You're looking fancy."

"Fancy is relative my friend. I just spent two weeks in the jungle followed by nearly two weeks at sea sleeping on a narrow bunk in a metal room that reminds me of a jail cell…except, of course, for the constant motion, the noise of the pump and the rumble of the engine. The trip wasn't altogether unpleasant. The company's been good. The scenery's been divine—at least during the rain forest part of the expedition—and I'm absolutely applauding myself for not getting seasick. I haven't had a cigarette for a month and I believe I'm going to stay quit; I feel perfectly marvelous. But as someone raised in the great indoors who's most perilous adventure prior to this was negotiating rush hour in Berlin, I'm going to pat myself on the back and go be proud of myself in a room at the Waldorf. You're welcome to join me but we're at the business stage of our operation. That means I get to return to a world *I* know how to navigate in. I intend to order a filet mignon tonight and a bottle of chilled wine, sleep in a fluffy bed and start my transition back into the realm of lawyers, accountants and businessmen. You, on the other hand, can be yourself, wear your work clothes—as long as we're not dining at the Ritz or enjoying a Broadway show—and be 'der little elf from der voods' who will impress our American customers."

A clanging sound resounded through the hull. Hanns and Werner came outside to the rail where a rumpled man with yellow teeth tottered on the dock accompanied by two large dogs.

"Whatcha doin' here? This is my goddamned dock."

Hanns winked at Werner whose face betrayed his disgust.

"I'm so sorry, my friend. I don't mean to trespass. Maybe we can come to some arrangement? Are you in charge of this pier?"

"I'm Burt. This is my goddamned dock. I lives in the warehouse here and don't like me no visitors."

"Burt, I need a place to tie my ship for three or four weeks. I need some security. I'm willing to pay a fair rate."

Burt started to protest but checked himself as the realization dawned on him; he'd stumbled on an opportunity.

"Werner, give me a hundred dollar bill."

"Hanns, you must be…"

"Trust me. Give me the hundred."

Hanns stepped off onto the dock and put the bill in Burt's hand. "If we had an unlimited supply of these, we'd be over at the freight terminal. Don't think of this as a get-rich proposition, but I can give you a hundred bucks a week if you and your dogs'll keep strangers off my ship.

"And how d'ya know I won't jes' run off with yer money?"

"A man who cares for dogs keeps company that's better than most people. You wouldn't be taking in street mutts and trying to keep them fed if you were only living for yourself"

Burt softened. "I do love me dawrgs. Bes' friends Aye ever 'ad."

"Here's a chance to keep them in puppy chow a while." Hanns kneeled to allow the two dogs to tentatively sniff his hand.

"Them dawrgs don't take too quickly to mos' folks like they's doin' you."

"Dogs are superb judges of character; they can smell bad intentions behind the most polished of phony smiles. People should bring dogs to business meetings; we could get rid of all the lawyers."

Burt smiled a yellow-toothed smile. "Damn right...but you know, if the cops come 'round, I don't want to get meself in the middle o' nothin'..."

"We're carrying lumber. There's nothing illegal on board and I don't expect you to get between the cops and us. I'm keeping no secrets here. You'll see the cargo when we unload tomorrow. I'll leave our contact information taped to the door when we're not on board. If someone in a uniform shows up, I don't care if you know anything about us or not. I just want your dogs keeping an eye on things so we can come and go at night without worrying about someone else giving us problems. There won't be any action here."

"Me 'n me crew's got ye covered, then." Burt scratched the head of one of his drooling beasts who now sat panting beside him.

Hanns bowed politely. Burt sauntered off, staring at the hundred dollar bill as if the cash had somehow fallen from the sky.

Werner was indignant. "Are you totally nuts?"

"I've dealt with a few waterfront bums in my life. He'll pass out by sundown but his dogs won't drink and they'll keep an eye on him and on *Gift Horse,* too. We'd never get dockage anywhere for a hundred bucks a week, and he'll stay in line enough to make sure he gets his next payment. I guarantee you—a whole community of wretched refuse lives on the teeming shores here. Old Burt will let them all know we're not to be fucked with."

A black Cadillac pulled up to the base of the pier. A horn honked. Raquel opened the door and waved. Hanns and Werner walked toward the car accompanied by the two dogs.

Hanns embraced Raquel, then clapped twice at the dogs who trotted back down the dock toward the warehouse on cue.

"Hanns, I want you to meet a dear friend of my family." She motioned to the back seat where a bearded man smiled from beneath a black hat. "Hanns, Rebi Horowitcz. Rebi, my husband

Hanns, and this is Werner Hullsman; he's handling our business logistics."

"Shalom und velcome to New York," came the old man's coarse but friendly voice.

Hanns accepted the rabbi's hand. He couldn't help but notice a tattooed number escaping from the rabbi's shirt sleeve.

The driver motioned for Hanns and Werner to get in the car.

Sabbath

Werner and Hanns followed Raquel and Rebi Horovitcz through a glass door into a narrow storefront. A second door opened into a long workspace with a bay door at the back. A pile of rough two-by-fours lay stacked in the center of the room. A half-dozen sheets of plywood leaned against the wall.

"It isn't zo much, but zis is vat ve gott," explained the rabbi. "My wife's cousin had a painting business here. He got sick a few years ago. It's been empty ever since. Clean ze place up ven you're finished."

Hanns offered a small bow, not certain if the gesture was appropriate but imagining it was unlikely to offend. "Thank you, Rabbi—and once the workshop is set up, tell me if you need anything fixed, painted or fabricated."

Rebi Horovitcz raised a salt and paper eyebrow and smiled. "I vill. I certainly vill." An aged hand extended once more from beneath the black coat. Hanns squeezed the fingers firmly, grateful for the familiar gesture.

"Lawrence vill be here vith a truck in a few minutes but you must verk quickly."

Raquel stepped on Hanns's foot in time for him to suppress his question. "Thank you for everything, Rebi. The space is perfect."

The rabbi handed her the key, turned and exited through the front door where his driver waited.

"Sorry to spring the marriage thing on you, honey, but dating outside the faith is strictly verboten. Screwing around with Germans—even Germans born *after* World War II ended—is a hair short of heresy. Of course, you can imagine my reputation for pushing boundaries but a lot of people in our community here were liberated from the death camps; they don't distinguish between 'old' Germans and 'new' Germans. Marrying a gentile is frowned upon but once done, the crime is considered to be successfully committed. You get a small chance to redeem yourself because whether anyone approves or not, you're surgically grafted onto the family. If we were 'just dating,' the lectures, guilt-trips and sabotage attempts would be absolutely epic. Let's be married; things will go much easier."

"Raquel, the chances of me successfully pretending to be a Hasidic Jew are about the same as the chances of me successfully parting the Red Sea. I don't know the first thing…"

"Don't pretend anything. Be friendly. Be yourself; you'll be fine."

"But these people are going to think I'm some sort of monster. Here I am with my blue eyes and blonde hair. I look like a poster boy for the Hitler youth."

"You may get some cold, icy stares from a few people; I can't help that, but the majority of us read about Nazi Germany in our school history books."

"Raquel, I grew up playing in the ruins of a war that ended before I was born. I remember being warned not play with unexploded shells and to stay away from damaged buildings but I sprang up with the wildflowers growing through the rubble. As a kid, I thought the destruction was a big mystery; it might as well have happened in medieval times. I experienced growth and rebirth, old buildings being torn down, new ones being built. They told me we lost a war. Most people were quietly introspective about what happened. Some never knew about the death camps. Some preferred to believe they didn't know about them. Some never said anything because they didn't want to get shot. I met my share of patriotic old Nazis but once you participate in murdering people—including children—on an industrial scale, hanging onto your old beliefs is probably easier than facing your own internal judgment. I'm not forgiving anyone for the horrible crimes they committed, but..."

"You're not in a position to have to forgive yourself or anyone else, or to have to ask anyone to forgive you. I can't promise you won't need to explain yourself to a few people, but the fact that I married you will stabilize things. What I always wondered is what would have happened if Hitler had been able to mobilize his nationalist campaign without making an internal enemy of the Jews? He stole a lot of assets but he destroyed a lot of talent and diverted a lot of energy. I wonder if Germany's Jews would have supported the Motherland and put their backs and brains and resources behind their country's expansion efforts. But we'll never answer that question. Jews were prohibited from buying Adolf's propaganda; they were made the brunt of it. If, instead, they'd been encouraged to support their country like every other German, would they have resisted or become one of the Reich's most formidable weapons? The question is not so much about the character of the Jewish people as about the character of humanity."

Werner stepped in. "In case you're wondering, my father wasn't in the Gestapo or anything. The army sent him off to Switzerland at the beginning of the War where he spent his time negotiating shipments of food and supplies from a safe, neutral place. He was lucky enough never to fire a shot and never to get fired at. The business connections he made helped him get set up after the war. When the fighting ended, the country lay in ruins. He knew how and where to get what needed to be gotten. I can't promise he knew nothing about the camps, but he was never assigned to a guard tower at Bergen Belsen.

"My personal history is like Hanns's. We were part of a new generation growing up in a new Germany. All we really saw of Hitler's world were ruins being bulldozed and paved over and occasional live ordnance removal teams."

Raquel took both of their hands. "This Jewish princess is proud of her German husband and friends. We're all good people. Everything will work out brilliantly."

"Raquel?" A deep voice echoed through the doorway. A large, smiling man wearing jeans and a Rolling Stones t-shirt under a prayer shawl and a bobby-pinned-on yamaka entered the work-space. "I'm Larry. My truck and my crew are parked outside. Let's get moving and get your cargo unloaded before we run out of time to work."

Hanns looked confused and decided to risk sounding ignorant. "And the hurry is?"

"Sundown; Friday; the Sabbath." Larry laughed. "Jews follow the world's most complicated, crazy and convoluted book of rules but there's a lot of joy and wisdom behind it. You'll pick it up."

"I'm Hanns. This is Werner. Let's grab a few sheets of that plywood to take with us. The planks on the dock are all either questionable or missing. We'll use the wood to cover the bad spots."

After bouncing a few miles downhill in a small moving truck, Hanns escorted Larry and a half dozen other large men down the dock, introducing them to the dogs on the way. Within two hours they had packed the truck to a point where four of the men had to hail a taxi to get back to the shop.

"That ought to get you going for now. We'll come back for the rest on Sunday morning. See you on the pier at seven o'clock."

Werner shook Larry's hand. "What do we owe you? You've been a tremendous help."

"Our pleasure. Just take good care of Raquel; Rabbi's orders. *Shabbat shalom.*" Larry disappeared. Hanns heard the truck lurch off to race the sun back to its parking place.

Hanns clapped his hands. "Thanks to 'Hebrews with Handtrucks,' we're in business. They were amazing. Tomorrow, I'm going to…"

Raquel squeezed his fingers.

"Tomorrow, you're gong to relax. No driving. No working. No sanding. Nothing electrical. Nothing technological. Nothing at all but eating and sleeping. You haven't taken a day off since the day you went up into the jungle at *Morne Diablotin* to look at trees—over a month ago. Werner, you're not doing much better. Tonight is Friday night. The sun is setting. *Shabbat Shalom.*"

Open for Business

"WERNER, you're brilliant. If we get half as many responses from people who want to buy the wood as we got from people who want to sand it, we'll be rich overnight."

"I'm amazed, myself. All I did was place a twenty-five dollar classified ad but I guess enough people read the paper to make it pull. I heard about a guy once who put a one-line ad in the paper: 'Foolproof business advice guaranteed to make you money: send $20 to such-and-such address.' Apparently, he got several thousand responses and to each, he sent back a note saying 'buy low, sell high.' Classified advertising works."

"Ah, life in the big city. I think I'm good for maybe a few weeks of this before I go home to the jungle to climb a tree."

"You'll get used to it. Urban life has its merits. Anyway Hanns, tomorrow there'll be eight people sanding away on the wood. I got two extra sanders in case one dies or we need more help."

"Good. The part where I'm stuck is on getting these things finished. I tinkered with a few varnish and epoxy samples, but the wood is freshly cut—still wet. No matter what I use, the moisture in the grain fogs the finish. I tried preparing the surface with

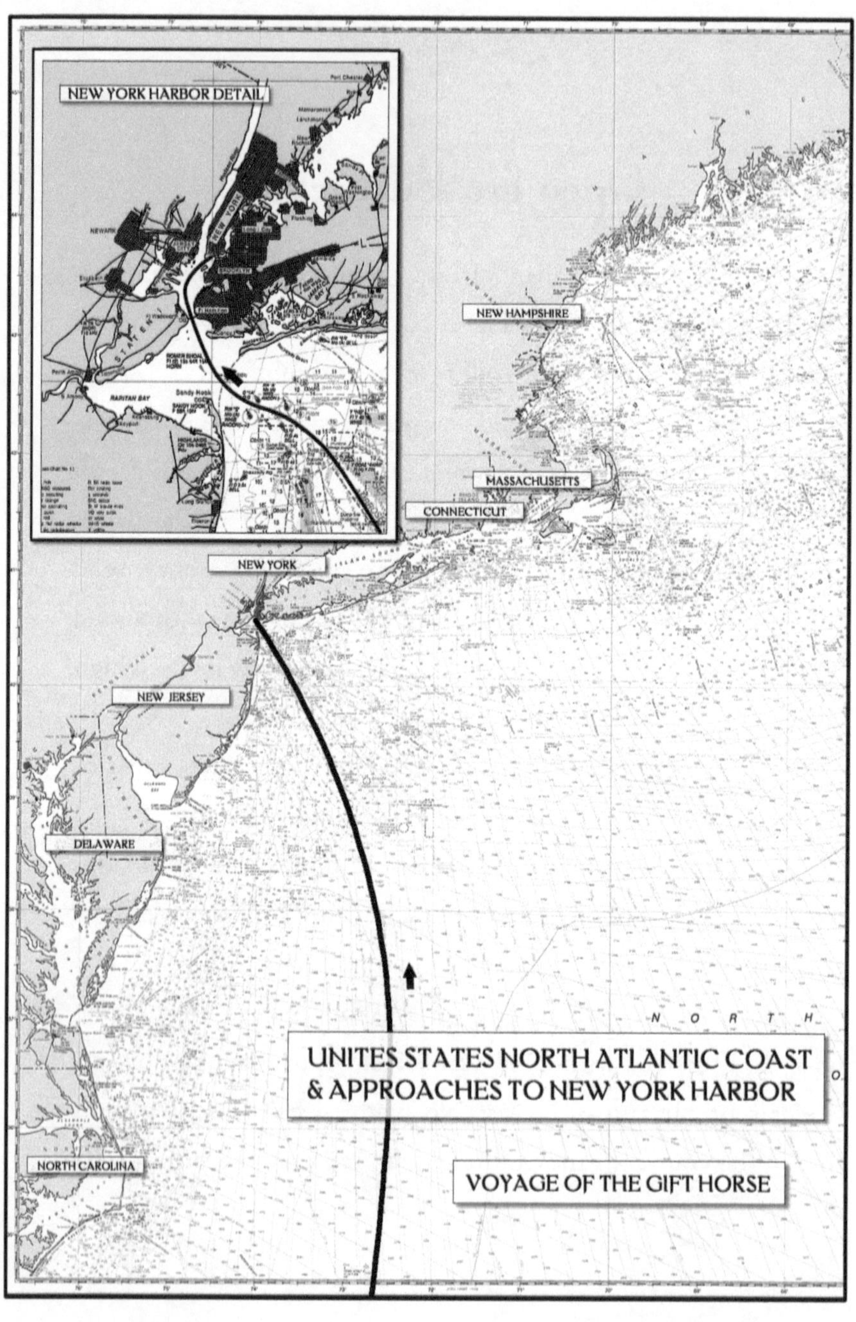

NEW YORK HARBOR DETAIL
NEW HAMPSHIRE
MASSACHUSETTS
CONNECTICUT
NEW YORK
NEW JERSEY
DELAWARE
NORTH CAROLINA
NORTH
UNITES STATES NORTH ATLANTIC COAST
& APPROACHES TO NEW YORK HARBOR
VOYAGE OF THE GIFT HORSE

various solvents but nothing's working out quite right yet. They make casting resins you can pour on that dry like liquid glass; I need to find some way to keep them from interacting with the water in the wood."

"Perhaps I can be of some assistance?" A thin man in casual business attire entered the door. "I'm usually polite enough to knock but I heard you talking and thought I'd leverage my dramatic timing instead." The man smiled. "I'm Dave Cohen. Rebi Horovitcz told me what you were doing. I'm a chemist; I developed a finish I'm in the process of selling to 3M—a two-part polyurethane that's water-based. I manufacture the stuff and sell batches to a few furniture companies to support my research but the product is not yet commercially available on any large scale. Other people have this same problem; they either wait months or years for the wood to dry or they kiln-dry the lumber, which can affect the wood structurally and requires some expensive equipment. My finish drinks the water and stays clear. Try a sample?" Cohen held out two small paint cans.

Raquel laughed. "Good to see you again, Dave. I knew you were a chemist but I had no idea what you were working on."

"Things are no different here than in the wilderness, Hanns; you need something and the Universe provides."

Hanns took a slab of wood from one of the tree slices that cracked during transport. Dave grabbed Werner's paper coffee cup from one of the plywood work tables, dumped the last half-inch of liquid into the trash can and swabbed the old coffee out with a paper towel. He poured equal parts from the two cans into the cup and mixed them with a screwdriver.

"Remember, the coating is water-based," said Cohen. "Just rinse off the screwdriver in the sink before the finish kicks off."

Hanns poured the honey-like liquid over the piece of wood and watched for signs of fogging. "Good so far. How long does this stuff take to cure?"

"The surface will cure to the touch in an hour or so. It'll be fairly durable in twenty four hours. In a week, the varnish will be pretty much indestructible. In your case, the finish will be going on fairly thick so you might want to wait forty-eight hours before actually selling a piece to anyone. However, you can put the entire finish on in a single application; no need to sand and wait between coats like you do with spar varnish."

"And you can supply me with this in quantity?"

"I have a warehouse full of five-gallon buckets and a big batch of some thicker stuff I've had a hard time getting rid of. My furniture customers prefer a thinner, sprayed-on finish."

Werner pulled out his cheque book. "How soon can you get two-hundred-fifty gallons here?"

"This afternoon if you want."

"And you'll take it back if it fogs up?" Hanns looked at Cohen.

"My finish won't fog up; I guarantee it."

By the end of the week, several hundred perfectly-finished table tops leaned against the walls of the store-front area and the back of the warehouse. Once finished, the wood of the *gommier* trees revealed a symphony of powerful reds, browns, yellows and beiges."

Werner patted his pocket. "The first dozen flew out the door at $500. I think we should raise our prices."

Hanns turned his palms upward, shrugged and smiled. "I'm going to pull out a few of the big, exceptional slices from near the bottom of the tree. Let's make those the 'Holy Grail' pieces at $2500. The rest, we can grade according to size and aesthetics. Some of the paintings going on in the wood grain should be in a museum."

By the end of the following week, Werner handed Hanns a wad of cash. "I'm more than paid off on my initial investment. Here's your first cut of the profits—$40,000. We'll sell the rest as fast as we can finish them and push them out the door."

"Two or three more weeks will do, Werner. I don't think this would have been any easier if we'd set up our own press to print the money but I owe a lot of that to you. I usually try to do everything myself."

"That's the difference between us, Hanns. You're a one-man industry; I'm an industrialist."

Raquel joined the celebration and put an arm around each of them. "I know this is going to disappoint Werner but now that our pockets are stuffed with a little cash and things are running smoothly, you and I should fly back to Dominica to make sure *Chaos* is floating straight and level. Werner, you're running the business end and at this point, production seems to be running on its own. If you can do without a few days of moral support, a quick trip to check on our home would be a good idea."

Werner turned to face Hanns. "She's right. You've been off your boat for over a month. You'd do well to make sure the locals see some lights on once in a while. Dominica seems like an honest enough place but if *Chaos* begins to appear abandoned..."

"We won't be gone too long—probably not more than a week. I don't want to leave you stuck here with a derelict freighter to take care of, either. I'll send you a postcard."

"Gee, thanks...and Hanns, I set up an account for us. I can't say I've been as conscientious as I should be about depositing all the cash but maybe we can get over to the bank today so you can both get your signatures on the account?"

Early the next morning, Hanns awoke to the sound of a metallic knocking on *Gift Horse's* hull. He dressed quickly and opened the metal door.

A man in a wrinkled uniform stood on the dock smoking a cigarette. "Good morning. You da Captain o' dis here vessel?"

"Yes, sir. What can I do for you?"

"I'm Fiorello. I'm from da Port Aut'ority. How long you been here?"

"A few days. Shouldn't be too much longer. Any problem?"

"You can't just come into New Yawk City and tie up anywheres you like."

"Why not? As far as I could tell, this is abandoned and neglected. You're not going to charge me dockage for *this* are you? I think the boat in front of me has been sitting on the bottom for years."

"This place is a safety hazard; you shouldn't be here but I ain't tryin' to collect rent or nuttin'. NYC is a major seaport. Don' matter to me if you ties up to a commercial pier, the Statue of Liberty or da town dump but you gotta pay port charges, buddy. Whatcha haulin' here anyways?"

"The cargo *was* lumber but everything's unloaded. You're welcome to come aboard. I can show you paperwork for everything."

"That's okay...just get over to the port office, check in and get on wit' yer business. Between you and me, I t'ink you done a smart thing. Long's you don't make this no permanent home, it'll be a while 'fore anyone gets 'round to hasslin' you 'bout tyin' up here. The Port Authority just' worries 'bout who comes in and outta da harbor. It's the City what worries 'bout the docks and who's doin' what on public property and they gots their hands full wit' bigger problems than you. Der was a guy here once lived on the bridge o' dat sunk freighter in front o' youse for two years, 'n' I know you must've met Louie an' his dogs. He's been here forever—sweet guy when he's sober. If your ship was all nice 'n shiny, you can bet someone'd be down here bustin' your wallet, but dey prob'ly ain't even noticed you. I ain't gonna blow the whistle on ya, but stay outta trouble if you's gonna play dis game. Don't get hurt on these old docks and don't get involved with nuttin' you shouldn't be doin'. If'n you don't make no trouble, you'll be okay here for a while."

"I appreciate you coming down. I didn't mean to cause any problems…"

"Just get down to the port and check in, okay buddy?"

"Yes, sir. Thanks for the heads up."

Fiorello strutted back down the dock. Hanns went back inside.

"Who was that, sweetie?" asked Raquel.

"Girl scouts. I ordered you two boxes of thin mints. Are you all packed and ready? We should try to be at the airport by 10:30 which means we need to be out of here in a half-hour."

A Home Ashore

Commonwealth of Dominica - June, 1978

RAQUEL hiked up the hill to where Hanns stood under the tall, lush canopy of the rain forest. "Honey, I..."

"Now, this is exciting. I'm going to build the main house here overlooking the stream and on the roof, and I'm going to build a big covered balcony where we can enjoy the vista of the Caribbean across the valley. So far, I've found mango, bananas, coconuts, papayas and callalou growing here and there's a flat place at the top near the cliff where we can put a vegetable garden. The tree house is going in right up there and I want to build a bat house to keep the mosquitoes..."

"... if we can close on the property."

Hanns put a hand on his hip. "What do you mean?"

"Jacques told me the cheque bounced."

"How's that possible? There should be a half-million dollars in the account. Did you call the bank?"

"Yeah, the account balance is about six grand. I also tried Werner at the shop and at his hotel; no answer."

"I don't know what's happening but don't worry too much. Werner's a business man but he doesn't have the guts or the heart to be a thief. Last week, he sent ten grand to a famine relief agency. Besides, why would he leave six thousand dollars in the account? If he was going to rip us off, he'd take everything."

"I know, but I don't want Jaques thinking we're flakes. Some other buyers were admiring his piece of land. I'd like to run down to the boat and give him cash for the property."

"Will that leave us with enough to..."

"Start building? Barely, but if we don't pay him soon, we won't own any land to build on and my heart is set on making our love nest here, man o' mine."

"Just do it. Let's make this happen. Everything's probably fine with Werner and if not, we've always gotten by so well on so little. If we find ourselves in a corner, we can sell *Chaos*. That will leave us with money to do whatever we want to do here."

"Hanns, you would part with *Chaos*?"

"I can't say selling her wouldn't put a tear in my eye, Raquel. I sailed thousands of miles in her and had some of the best and worst times of my life, but we're here; you're my adventure now. I'm happy, and by the way, I have no intention of taking this ring off. I'm yours, sweetheart."

"Yeah, I was thinking the same thing. I never thought our union would happen like this...but at the risk of screwing up a precious moment, before we go pay off our property and consummate this marriage, I don't wan't you to sell *Chaos* for this. I wouldn't ..."

"*Chaos* is a wonderful tool and she's full of amazing memories, but without adventurous people on board taking her to exotic places, she's a material object sitting on the water gathering marine life and rotting away. The worst thing you can do to a boat is let her sit idle in the water. Metal corrodes. Sails mold and deteriorate. Paint and varnish peel. Wood gets soggy and soft. You can store a boat in a boatyard for quite a while but if you leave her in the water, you have to care for her every day or she'll die quickly. You've been sailing long enough to see all the rundown boats and derelicts in every port. Every one of them was once shiny and new but most people are clueless about what goes into keeping a boat up. I'm compulsive about jumping on anything that breaks or wears out. Otherwise, I'll fall behind and never catch up. Boats are just things, even if they're part of a special category of things endowed with souls. I figure if we're going to be playing Tarzan and Jane up here in our jungle hideaway, all we need is a little open boat—if we own a boat at all. Once the house is built, if we get bored, we can buy another boat or build one ourselves. I don't want *Chaos* to die on my watch. If we keep her, I'll be working on her a day or two a week and spending money on her. It doesn't make any sense to maintain her unless we're using her."

"But it feels like the Lone Ranger selling Silver."

"We never heard what happened to Silver after the Lone Ranger got married and found someone else to ride all day. What you don't do with a good horse is lock him in a stable and pretend to love him by shoveling in hay and mucking his stall once a week. You honor that horse by letting him go and giving him to someone who wants to stay be in the saddle every day."

Raquel took a deep breath, inhaling the rain forest bouquet. "Well, let's get our business taken care of and have a little fun. Tomorrow, we've got to go back to Manhattan; this week went by in two days."

"I agree, and as far as *Chaos* goes, don't worry. If we do sell the boat, we'll need a little while to find the right buyer. I won't sell her to anyone who has the money, and whenever I sell a boat, I deliver her wherever the owner wants as part of the price. We'll get a farewell cruise to somewhere and as always, we'll make it an adventure."

"I'll look forward to that, Hanns.

"When we get back down to Portsmouth, you motor out to *Chaos* and get some cash for Jacques. I'll jump on the pay phone and try to scare up some information about Werner. Maybe the rabbi knows something?"

"Okay, Raquel, but afterward, I'm taking you to Roseau for a nice dinner and then home for dessert."

The Search

"No, his mother hasn't heard from him. She says he always calls her on Sundays and this is the second Sunday he's missed. The rabbi hasn't seen him and he hasn't been to the hotel. They didn't want to give me any information at first but one of the desk clerks recognized me and told me he hasn't been back for quite a while. All his stuff is still in his room; they're getting ready to dump it." Hanns took a sip of his tea. "Burt, the dog man on the dock, hasn't seen him either.

"This isn't like Werner; something happened to him. The shop is empty—too empty. Someone embezzling a half-million dollars wouldn't burden themselves with a pile of tools; they'd fly light with a backpack or a briefcase. And no way in hell would Werner Hermann spray-paint graffiti on the walls; Werner's a sharp guy with a lot of class. This is the work of someone psychotic and stupid and primitive. The money disappearing is an epic clusterfuck but I want to find out what happened to Werner."

Raquel sat on the work table. "I already called the police. They couldn't find anyone named 'Werner' in jail or in any other kind of trouble who matches his description. I did file a missing person report but probably, a hundred thousand missing people in New York City don't even know they're reported missing."

"And if the cops found a missing person with a half-mil in cash on them, I doubt that person or the money would ever show up," interjected Hanns. "Too much incentive to keep the cash and chuck the body down a manhole or something."

"Always the cynic, my dear. The police suggested I check the morgues. I'm a tough New York bitch but I'm going to pass on looking at bodies all day; I'll sleep better. Some people die pretty hard in the city."

"I can't say I'll enjoy that either but I got Werner into this thing. I'll get the phone book and find out where the body banks are. You go to the money bank and clean out the account before the cops decide our cash is evidence and lock us out. We've got to refuel *Gift Horse* and God only knows what other expenses we'll incur before this is over. I also want to paint over the graffiti on the inside of the shop and scrape the varnish drippings off the floor before we leave. Even if we got ripped off, I want to contain our misfortune and return this place in top condition.

"Good thing we were out of the country when this happened. Otherwise, my dear wife, we'd be suspect—and that would take us to an even deeper and shittier level of 'deep shit.'

"…And maybe somebody should fingerprint these empty bottles? I'm sure Werner Hermann was not drinking Miller beer."

The City of New York's Office of the Chief Medical Examiner was a failed attempt at architectural modernism squatting incongruously on First Avenue at the end of a long row of traditional brownstones—a windowless obelisk of beige brick sitting atop a small, flat rectangle of what appeared to be black air-conditioning vents. This structure perched above another boxy layer consisting of a series of aluminum-framed glass windows and doors inset with glossy gray panels framed by two unusual blue brick facades, one of which had brass lettering mounted on its front face. The morgue was three-and-a-half miles from the South Street Pier district but the walk gave Hanns time to think and marvel at the contrast between how people lived here in the City and how they lived in the volcanic jungles of Dominica. Hanns guessed the top floor was probably a gigantic refrigerator. He steeled himself for what he might encounter inside. Under the best of circumstances, he'd look at a few corpses and come up empty-handed. *Werner, if you show up at the shop with a big smile on your face, you may wind up in the morgue anyway by the time I'm done with you.*

Inside, he stepped up to a window and waited for a fat woman behind the desk to notice him. He coughed once and got no response. Finally, he rang the handbell on the window counter. "Excuse me, miss. I need to..."

"Just wait a minute."

Hanns thought better of overtly protesting the clerk's lack of acknowledgement. Instead, he made disgusting post-nasal drip sounds. "I'm sorry," he explained in mock apology. "My sinuses are acting up."

"How can I help you, sir." The woman looked irritated to have been disturbed from whatever it was she wasn't doing.

"I'm looking for a missing person. I thought…"

"Have you filed a missing person report with the NYPD?"

"Yes, ma'am."

She handed Hanns a form on a clipboard with a filthy pen scotch-taped to a piece of string tied to the clip. Hanns skimmed the document. The text was mostly legalese having to do with the confidentiality of the people whose bodies he might be viewing. On a second sheet, he answered a few questions about race, gender, hair color, identifying marks, clothes the person was last seen in, etc. *I wish he wasn't so damned nondescript, Why couldn't he have a tattoo that said 'Gladys' or an odd streak of white in his beard?* Werner Hermann was so ordinary in appearance, Hanns could hardly imagine what he looked like. "Extremely ordinary-looking," he wrote in the comment box. "Probably dressed in slacks and a button-up shirt, possibly a sport jacket. Clean-cut but not meticulously so."

He handed the form to the obnoxious clerk and sat down on a hard bench next to a table full of several-month-old magazines.

He skimmed through *Cosmopolitan* out of sheer curiosity but the glossy fashion photos made him feel that much farther away from his home planet. He switched to a *National Geographic* featuring an article about North Sea Oil. The ticking of the second hand on a white-faced institutional clock grew louder as the minutes passed.

After twenty minutes, a door opened. A white-haired man in a lab coat appeared. "You're Hanns?"

"Yes, sir."

"Been to a morgue before?"

"I've been damned close many times but always seemed to find an excuse not to come at the last second."

The man didn't smile. "Follow me."

They entered a claustrophobic elevator that smelled faintly of formaldehyde. One of the florescent lights above its yellowed plastic ceiling panels flickered and buzzed annoyingly.

"I'm afraid we keep the temperature on the chilly side. I can get you a lab coat but it won't help very much," offered the orderly.

"Thanks. I'll deal with the cold."

"You know, some of what you're going to see may not be pretty if you're not used to..."

"I understand, but I'd rather suffer a little discomfort than get used to it."

They entered a large room. One side offered a row of stainless steel tables and sinks; the opposite wall presented an array of small, square doors across an industrial green linoleum floor. After looking at his clipboard, the orderly opened door number 68. He lifted up a sheet to expose a pair of tagged feet which he compared to his notes before sliding the cadaver out and pulling back the sheet to reveal the face."

"Nope. Glad he's still smiling, though. Probably died in the saddle."

The orderly cracked the faintest of smiles and moved on.

Two more doors yielded nothing familiar.

When the last door opened, Hanns knew as soon as the feet were uncovered. "You found him."

"How do you know?"

"I don't know how I know; I just know. Let's see him."

The orderly pulled back the sheet.

"Jesus, Werner. What the hell happened to you? How did you wind up here?"

Hanns forgot how cold the room was.

The man in the lab coat went to a file cabinet and matched the number on Werner's tag. "Apparently, he fell from a fifteenth floor balcony."

"But he looks fine, almost like he's asleep."

"Aside from some bruising, he's in decent shape on the outside, but he's a sack of broken bones and ruptured organs on the inside. The toxicology report says he was full of speed. Some of these brainracers think they can fly. A few try. They wind up here every so often."

"Speed? Werner? This doesn't make any sense. He must have been set up. Someone drugged him up and pushed him off."

"I'm sorry. That kind of thing does happen but only rarely. More often, people have a secret life; a bad habit or a weak spot that catches up with them. I'm not saying you're wrong, but I'm pretty sure the Justice Department is going to file this as a drug-induced suicide and not pursue the matter. Unless you have a really solid suspect, my advice to you is to let it go, too. Cases like this suck away the lives of good people who would be better off moving on."

Hanns took a deep breath. The morgue felt cold after all. "Goodbye, Werner."

"I'm sorry this isn't a happy time but I'll need you to fill out some paperwork so we can get your friend home to his family."

"Sure. It's the least I can do. Thanks."

"But Hanns, we have to find out who did this. We owe it to Werner."

"Raquel, I'm not any happier about the situation than you are. Werner was a friend—not to mention we just lost all the money we needed to cruise in style for the rest of our lives—but look at the various scenarios and think about them from a risk-return standpoint:

"Was Werner a secret speed freak? That theory is low on the list of possibilities but if it's the case, the money's out on the streets. An investigation will take weeks, put us in touch with a lot of dangerous and unsavory people and most likely bag us nothing but trouble.

"Did someone in the Jewish community see the money coming in and get greedy or have some kind of grudge against a German…?"

"Hanns! No way…"

"I didn't say that's what happened but a detective would ask the same questions. Who knew what was going on? Who had access? Who had any possible motive? I'm not saying Werner was murdered by a Jewish conspiracy, but if one person…anyway… let's continue….

"Most likely, someone came in posing as a customer. Mr. X watches hundred dollar bills flying over the counter. Maybe he strikes up a conversation? Werner doesn't have any friends here; he's lonely. He accepts a social invitation and boom—no more cash and no more Werner. Nobody broke into the shop; whoever did this got the key from Werner, opened the door and cleaned the place out.

Raquel nodded.

Hanns continued. "So, if the cash is on the streets, write it off. In the unlikely case Werner's murder was an inside job, we can conclude there *is* a Jewish Mafia; I wouldn't mess with them for ten times what we lost. Meanwhile, we—actually, *you*—the boat's in your name—have an illegally docked freighter on the South Street Pier. We could get the cops involved but I didn't even clear Customs until I flew back from Dominica with you two days ago; We'd have to deny I was even here before two days ago. I don't want our story to unravel. Immigration might open up a new bag of problems over money we can't recover and a friend we can't bring back from the dead.

"Of course I want to find out what happened, but curiosity killed the cat. I say let's clean up our mess and get the hell out of here."

Two days later, *Gift Horse* slipped quietly out of New York Harbor bound for San Juan, Puerto Rico where her new Haitian owners awaited.

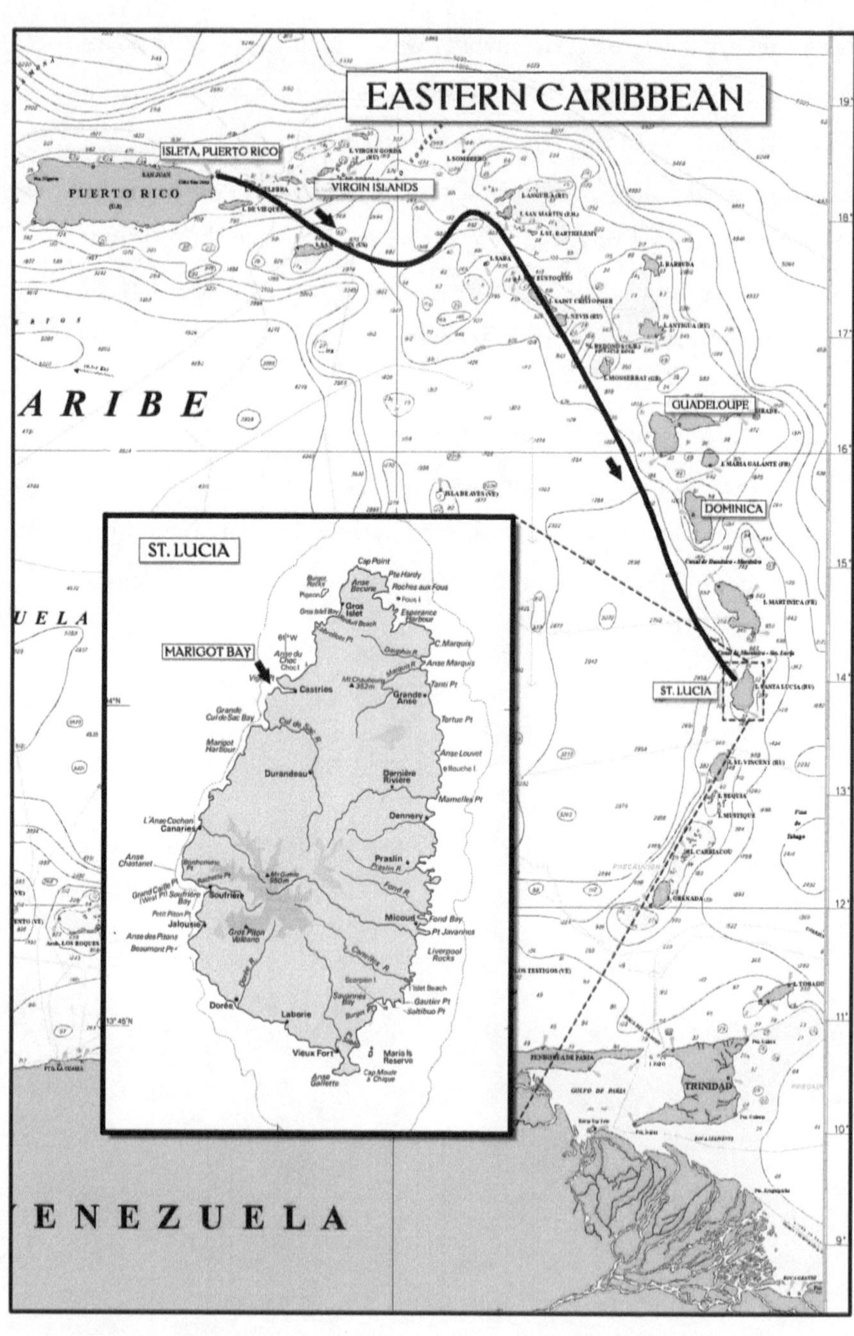
EASTERN CARIBBEAN
ISLETA, PUERTO RICO
VIRGIN ISLANDS
PUERTO RICO
GUADELOUPE
DOMINICA
ST. LUCIA
ST. LUCIA
MARIGOT BAY
Castries
Gros Islet
Grande Anse
Dennery
Praslin
Micoud
Vieux Fort
Laborie
Dorée
Soufrière
Canaries
Durandeau
ENEZUELA
ARIBE

Final Passage

Isleta, Puerto Rico–November, 1978

"Don't be sad, my dear. This is the best part of boat ownership. We just flew through a Lloyds of London survey; the boat is in the best shape she's ever been in. Now we get to sail someone else's boat, set up exactly how we like, to a beautiful place, hang out for a few days and walk away. The goddamned Royal Navy doesn't get a thumbs-up from Lloyds on the first pass; we got a perfect survey except for two fifty-nine-cent hose clamps. Our pockets are full and *Windship Chaos* is going to a loving home. Whatever our Canadian doctor couple may lack in boat-building skills, they make up for in being able to afford to have things done right. *Chaos* will be cruised and cared for. We'll find our own, smaller boat soon enough and from what I hear, St. Lucia is gorgeous."

"I've always thought of her as our home together. I'm struggling with the idea of someone else sailing her away."

"Well, funny how your time on *Windship Chaos* began and ended here in Isleta. At least you're getting a full circle experience."

"I suppose. So, are we ready to put her back in the water?"

"The sea is where she's happiest.

"Are you okay with dumping the Dominica property so soon, Raquel? We had our hearts set on..."

"I'm still skeptical but we had an adventure and got our money out. I'm willing to gamble on your instincts; I've known you long enough to trust them. Time will tell if we made the right decision."

"If your investor friend is right, when Dominica goes independent from Britain, foreigners will have a tough time verifying their property ownership with the new government. Also, in any kind of major hurricane, our land could come sliding down the mountain as a heap of mud—and I overlooked the possibility of earthquakes or volcanic activity. I felt bold when we bought it—I thought we might settle down in the rain forest—but the more energy we invested, the less ready we were to get out of harm's way. I kept missing *Chaos* and the mobility we had with her. I can't say I'm being entirely rational but in my gut, I think we made a smart move.

"The only downer is we can't back out of our deal with *Chaos's* new owners. I would much rather pick up where we left off."

Hanns descended the ladder, walked over to the boatyard office to pay his bill and told the manager he was ready to launch.

An hour later, *Chaos* blasted southeast, taking advantage of a northerly set to the easterly winds. "Let's enjoy this cruise, take our time and not beat ourselves up. When the wind is right, we sail. When it's not, we'll anchor in the lee of the islands and wait for the weather to change. I told the Connors we weren't going to do this trip on any kind of ridiculous schedule."

Six days later in the early afternoon, Hanns sighted the entrance to Marigot Bay. "Once we get a bit farther south, we should see a small forest of masts in the harbour. Usually, these islands have their little inlets and lagoons on the eastern side where you wouldn't want to get caught between the weather and the shore. The constant pounding of winds and seas over the millennia makes these coasts rocky and steep. Here, due more, I suspect, to volcanic activity, St. Lucia has a natural inlet on the Caribbean side with mountains all around. Marigot Bay is a famous hurricane hole and of course, a whole industry sprang up to serve the yachtsmen. I can't say they're not smart to take advantage of its popularity, but paradise found is usually paradise lost."

"The island is certainly beautiful, like a scene from the South Pacific with the coconut palms and mountains. You'd think we'd be immune to being impressed by exotic, tropical islands after living in Dominica for four months."

"I'm happy we're not. As a species, we're tremendous stimulus-seekers; of course, I'm nobody to point a finger. A fish can swim around a tank for years by itself and as far as we can tell given its lack of capacity for expression, it can be perfectly happy as long as it's fed and the water is clean. Ironically, *homo sapiens* is endowed with a tremendous capacity for boredom. At the same time, we're driven by an innate desire to seek meaning. Most people choose an off-the-shelf system for determining *meaningfulness* so they can focus on finding palliatives for the boredom—usually a stream of new toys, lovers, locales and experiences. Others view outward interaction with the world as an endless and illusory cycle of meaningless stimulus pursuits that never offers anything other than momentary relief from the mind's constant, infantile desires for the more and the new. In English, this means too many people get bored with paradise; they end up building on top of it or drinking too much. When I feel the Caribbean's magic, I know I haven't lost my own.

"Can you harden up the starboard jib sheet for me?"

"Of course." Raquel inserted the handle in the winch and cranked the line in a few turns. "You were saying?"

"I like to work the problem from both ends. I appreciate and even admire people who are able to quiet their minds and focus on living a more spiritual life. Whether or not you agree with them, you'll find this group to be one of the least violent and most compassionate, tolerant and intellectual communities of people on Planet Earth. At least they're not running around bothering me with their personal perspectives on truth.

"I can tell you of a few times in my life when I regretted being seduced by something shiny and new and exotic and sexy, but

I often wonder if, with few exceptions, the self-proclaimed followers of the inner path aren't substituting an abstract object of spiritual desire for the transient objects of corporeal desire? If spirituality means training your mind to want enlightenment more than food, orgasms or a new stereo system, I don't think it has much to offer. I guess enlightenment has some value as far as getting people off the consumer bandwagon, but the ironic nature of enlightenment is the more you want it, the farther away it gets—like trying to fall asleep; the harder you try, the more familiar you get with the patterns in the ceiling tiles.

"So, for me, most of the spiritualists are playing the same game. I just like them better because the nature of their game discourages them from disrupting my own party. But beyond my few regrets, I cherish some fantastic memories of being seduced by things that were shiny, new, exotic and sexy; I hope to accumulate more of those."

Raquel laughed. "I like when you get on a philosophical roll, especially when you're not crucifying the last idiot you encountered. Do continue."

"Thank you, my dear, for the encouragement. So, humans innately pursue things that trigger the brain's pleasure receptors, and those sensory systems are cross-wired so we can receive pleasure from any combination of them, or even from the mere imagining of stimulus. We come off the assembly line addicted to our own endorphins. We don't crawl around very long before we figure out some things are scary and uncomfortable, other things are reassuring and comforting, and a few are fucking fantastic. I think it's quite natural to become aware of yourself as an experiencing being and to try to live closer to the pleasure side of the equation, which is why, even in my humble style, I enjoy my life of pleasurable indulgence."

"Yes, but you're baiting me. You're not a run-of-the-mill materialist, either."

"You know me too well. I love great sex, great food and great new places, and I like a certain amount of variety in all these things but having equipped myself to live as I do, I'm happy. I aspire, however, to be a gourmet of sorts with respect to what I consume in the world. The material things I enjoy most are almost exclusively tools that facilitate some measure of self-expression or save me time I can dedicate later to the appreciation of more brain candy. I'm a social creature but I limit my circles to exclude people who arrive with too much baggage. Locked up in a cell by myself, I'd probably choose the 'inner path' but I've been able to arrange to live in a way where I get significantly more than the recommended daily allowance of positive stimulus; my happiness gauge isn't screaming at me to change course. I sail the Caribbean; I eat fresh mangos and papayas; I used to fly airplanes and race cars; I climb around in the rain forest, enjoy an array of talented and interesting friends and a life of adventure. I believe in a middle ground where we can cultivate a habit of not acting impulsively every time the mind screams for something new. But instead of suppressing all desire, why not embark on a life full of joy and fresh experience? My spirituality is not concerned with trying to get to a certain place or state; I'm not trying to get away from one either. The only quasi-spiritual exercise I do is to try to remind myself to return to what I call 'movie camera mode.'"

"I do that too, Hanns, though I never put the idea into words before. I'm a sophisticated human camera; the film is running; I record light and sound and experience. The movies come in; I process them and react to them. Sounds and gestures issue from me automatically in response."

"Exactly, and this deeper part of you—maybe it's the invisible 'nothing and everything' you find when you lick down to your metaphorical lollipop stick—is somehow beyond all stimulus and reaction. *Something* is experiencing all that brain chatter; you can find that something by being aware of your own awareness of the moment as easily as you can by disciplining yourself to ignore the chatter altogether. The *you* who's an observer is distinct from a deeper *you* you can never observe directly—who's more like a film archivist or projectionist. One you projects; the other you watches the movie."

"Whenever something scary or unpleasant happens, I try to retreat to my 'movie' perspective so I can process things in smaller pieces, one 'frame' at a time. Then, I look at the millions of films sitting in my library and I remind myself that whatever I'm struggling with will inevitably land in the archive like all the previous experiences. It's only a matter of time before I load new film and point my camera at something more pleasant."

"Well, my dear Raquel, I'm afraid I've found something truly scary for you to point your camera at. See the blonde riding on the bow of the ketch coming out of Marigot harbor? Remember Yvonne, the one I told you about? Meet Sister Goldenhair Surprise."

The girl on the ketch looked at the oncoming trimaran. Her friendly smile of yachting camaraderie turned to horrified recognition. She scrambled back to the cockpit and went below deck, out of site.

An Old Friend

Hurricane Hole Bar–Marigot Bay, St. Lucia

"We cruised *Windship Chaos* together for two years; she jumped on board in Jacksonville, Florida. We sailed all through the Bahamas and almost got killed more than once trying to get down to the Turks and Caicos. We had a perfect romance and partnership and some incredible adventures. Everything was happiness and bliss until one day I caught her using the ship's radio to send out information about drug boats. Turned out she was some sort of DEA secret agent; she'd been using me and *Chaos* the entire time. I didn't want any part of that shit. When I found out, I booted her off the boat. I wanted to end our dealings peacefully, but… well…things ended badly. She tried to give me a goodbye hug and I freaked out. Part of me was angry and part of me thought she might actually try to kill me. You know I'm not a violent person, but after two years of being played, I lost my…I…."

"That's over. Don't explain yourself. You're not gonna lose your cool on me and I'm not pretending to be someone I'm not; we're the 'real deal.' I'm sorry you had to cross paths with her again."

"Can I get you something from the bar, my dear, maybe one of those frozen coconut drinks?"

Raquel licked her lips. "I'm relaxed. I had a hot shower and a good nap. We had a perfect trip. St. Lucia is beautiful. Our bank account is huge by our standards. Sure; why the hell not? I'd love a frozen coconut drink, and if you don't mind, some of those coconut shrimp, too."

"Coming right up…and Raquel?"

"Yes."

"As we close our chapter on *Chaos,* I want to say you've been the perfect person to share these incredible experiences with. I've never been happier."

She blew him a kiss. Hanns strode off to the tiki bar where he sat down to wait for the bartender's attention which was fixed on a rather drunk young woman wearing a tied-on skirt and a loose bikini top.

A couple sat down at the adjacent bar stool. Hanns recognized her scent immediately, something he'd never consciously noticed or forgotten before that now, in its sudden reappearance, struck him as old, familiar and uncomfortable. He took a deep breath and spoke in a penetrating almost-whisper. "Hi. Remember me?"

Yvonne turned, trying to compose herself. "You're still here? What are you doing still…"

"What's it to you, bitch?"

Yvonne's companion, a large man with a military chin stood up. "How dare you talk to the lady like that? You..."

"Get out of my way or I'll knock you down." Hanns's face went red. "I'm going to have a brief conversation with my old friend. You don't want me getting in your face or making any noise about your *secret mission* here. Do you read me?"

Confronted by Hanns's enormous presence and not wanting to have their operation compromised, the man stepped aside and hovered at the end of the bar where he could monitor Yvonne from outside the circle of confrontation.

"I'll keep this brief. Up until a few seconds ago, I carried guilt feelings about the way we parted company but now I have to thank you. When you asked why I was still here, you reaffirmed something I never quite wanted to believe about what you people are actually capable of. I don't know what was supposed to happen to me as punishment for discovering what you were made of but I promise you it didn't happen and it *won't.* Now, my only regret is that you weren't lost at sea when I had the chance to lose you. You vindicated me with one sentence."

Yvonne stared open-mouthed.

"One last question for you..."

Yvonne offered a faint nod.

"What the hell are *you* still doing here? Beat it! *Now!*"

Yvonne got up, gathered her companion and disappeared.

Hanns took a deep breath, paid the bartender and carried two frozen coconut shells back to the table where Raquel stared dreamily into a glass candle. "Did anything happen while I was gone?"

"Well, a guy saw me alone and came by to hit on me. I can't say he assured me he's much of a sailor but he's looking for crew to help him bring his boat to Puerto Rico—a 35-foot Herschoff, a classic wooden sloop. I told him we'll be carrying a heap of luggage from moving the last of our gear off *Chaos* but if he's willing to haul us and our stuff to Isleta, we'll come take a look tomorrow."

"Sounds good to me." Hanns took a sip and set his coconut mug down. "Half our lives are sitting in storage. I'm ready to split when the tide is right."

"Did you not like your drink?"

"It started off with this beautiful, tropical attitude but somehow, it isn't living up to my expectations."

Hitchhiking Home

"I'm Doug. Welcome aboard *Eris.* She's a bit rough around the edges but she's a good sailor—just a bit more than I'd care to handle myself."

Hanns and Raquel stepped aboard, introduced themselves and inspected the boat.

"How'd you guys end up looking for a ride in St. Lucia?"

"We just sold our big cruising trimaran. The new owners are on their way and we figured we'd rather sail back than fly. We have a lot of gear with us from moving off the boat and we'd prefer not to pay a bunch of penalties for overweight baggage. Mostly, we think sailing is more fun. We're always headed down-island, missing out on making the easy trip north with the wind behind us. How about you?"

"I was down in Trinidad and a guy approached me about running a few bales from St. Lucia to Florida. I never fancied myself a smuggler but the money was too good to pass up. I headed straight here but by the time I arrived, I'm not sure what happened. I either missed the connection or they got busted and shut down. So here I am, looking for someone to stand some watches and share expenses."

"It's just as well smuggling didn't work out for you. This place *definitely* has its share of DEA agents poking around. Also, I hear sometimes the dopers will plant bales of seeds and twigs on a handful of yachts and send them out as decoys. These poor bastards think they're going to make a fast buck until the real smugglers tip off the cops. You go off to jail over a few hundred pounds of ratty, worthless ganja and the Coast Guard and the DEA burn up their resources chasing crap."

"You know a lot about the drug running thing."

"The answer to your question is 'no.' We've been approached a few times but we've always kept our noses clean. If you spend any time sailing here, you'll find that in most places, the smugglers don't hide anything because the cops are well-paid to turn a blind eye. What's happening and where is fairly obvious, but you smile and mind your own business and you keep sailing. I know enough about drug-running to stay away from it. As a matter of fact, if you're…"

"No, no…just trying to get back to Puerto Rico to fix up the boat. I'm guessing since you recently sold one, you're familiar with navigating and setting sails and…?"

"We're old hands at cruising and I'm also a diesel mechanic. I've been sailing full-time for the last seven years.

"How soon are you leaving? Are you ready to go?"

Hanns's question caught Doug off-guard. "When?" he stammered. "You mean now?"

"We can have our stuff on board and stowed away in an hour. The boat and the schedule are yours but we're ready to go sailing."

"Hmm… yeah … I guess we could … I've got no reason to wait … sure."

At noon the next day, Hanns steered *Eris* into the lee of Dominica in a torrential downpour. The weather hadn't appeared at all threatening as they approached; Hanns and Raquel were taken by surprise when the wind disappeared and the rain came. As *Eris* had no Bimini top to shade or shelter her cockpit, their clothes were drenched, but reaching in the lee of the islands on an antique wooden boat was a delight. Hanns and Raquel laughed in the cockpit as the rain streamed down.

"Doug, would you like us to handle the anchors?"

"Sure. You guys are already wet."

Raquel drove the boat. Hanns tended the foredeck. This was an old drill for them by now; anchoring was fast and easy.

Having quickly cleated off the anchor, neatly furled the mainsail and lashed the jib on deck, Hanns stripped off his shirt. "Are you thinking what I'm thinking?"

Raquel reached through the companionway to where shampoo and soap gel sat on a shelf inside the bulkhead. On deck, she stripped off her clothes and squirted Hanns with soap. He laughed, filled a bucket with water streaming off the boom, and dumped it over her head. She squealed and spit a stream of fresh water back in his face. Their two naked figures danced with pure joy on the deck in the tropical rain.

"Doug, come grab a fresh water shower while you can."

"Goddamit! What the hell are you guys doing? You're gonna get the boat soaking wet!"

Hanns went back to the cockpit to glare at Doug through the companionway as rain poured from the sky and swirled down the cockpit drains. "I guess we're finished. I'm so sorry we got water on your boat. Are you totally fucking nuts or what?"

Doug glowered back. "I... I'm a Christian and..."

"Save yourself. We're *not* Christians, and if we were, we're married, and the bible doesn't say anything about showering naked with your wife in the rain. Get a life. Take a shower."

Raquel shot Hanns an eyebrow, quietly suggesting he step back from the futile confrontation. He composed himself.

"Doug, I'm sorry if we offended you. That wasn't our intention. She's your boat. Let us know how you want us to play. I'm sorry I got in your face."

On deck, Raquel nodded her approval and shot Hanns a look that implied, 'that's right; be nice and friendly to the psychotic man.'

That night, Hanns slept with his diving knife under his pillow.

The Reptile Brain

Three Days Later–Simpson Bay, Dutch St. Maarten

"It's a relief to have 'psycho man' off the boat for a few hours, and I love to get my pencil sharpened on a lazy Sunday morning. I wonder what a guy like Doug thinks about when he goes to church. Peace on earth? Good will toward men? Tolerance and forgiveness? Burning heretics at the stake?"

Raquel lay on top of Hanns, smiling from the morning's exertions and feeling the cool trade winds streaming through the hatch onto her naked body. "Go easy on Doug; he's a troubled soul."

"He's not a troubled soul; he's a biologically confused thirty-three-year-old adolescent. He's trapped in his own small cave with a dominant male and a sexy woman who's spoken for. He wants to be king in his own domain but I'm the one sleeping with the female and I'm a far more experienced sailor than he is. Moreover, I'm neither defending you nor challenging him. I'm not even copping on to the existence of biological forces at play. I'm sailing the boat with my wife—who's also doing a heck of a job sailing the boat by the way—and 'psycho man' is imploding because his reptile brain wants to lock horns with me to win a chance to mate with you. Since that's not working, and physically, he knows he can't overpower me, he finds all sorts of irrational faults with us and spends his time brooding."

"Speak of the devil. I hear the dinghy now. Maybe we should get dressed?"

"Fuck that. We're engaged in the most innocent and natural act in the world. How the hell does he think he got to this planet anyway? Let's close the bulkhead door and go another round."

"You, my dear, are an instigator. Once you're convinced you're right—and by the way, I think you're spot on—to hell with anybody who even thinks about denying you your rights. But it's always easier to humor a fool than to argue with him."

"Ah, Raquel, you know me too well...but this is such a delicious morning. I suppose you're right." Hanns grabbed for his jeans. Raquel searched the sheets for her panties.

A stern voice called from the cockpit. "What are you guys doing?"

"We're fucking our brains out. You ought to try some. It's good for you."

Raquel sighed and nodded. "Life with you is always an adventure. Here comes another one."

"You sinners; fornicating on the Lord's day! How dare you contaminate my home with your Satanic ways. Get out of here. Away! Get off my boat. I won't suffer blasphemy and obscenity aboard my..."

"Put a cork in that bottle. I'm not even going to argue about how stupid you sound telling a married couple they can't sleep together when they're alone on a sailboat in a tropical anchorage, *especially* on a Sunday. Get a life and stop judging lest ye be judged. Second, let me make things absolutely clear; you are *not* stranding my wife and me on a dock in St. Maarten with three hundred pounds of gear because you're not getting laid and can't handle having someone tell you how to navigate your boat properly. You offered us passage to Puerto Rico and you're damned well taking us to Puerto Rico. We can leave now and sail straight through if you want—Isleta is only 160 miles from here; you can get rid of us tomorrow night—but you're going to keep your commitment and take us there. You don't need to talk to us or like us or even look at us, but you're responsible for our passage. I paid our share of the expenses and that's as good as a ticket to me."

Doug gritted his teeth, jumped back into the dinghy and motored off toward shore at top speed.

"Hanns, was it absolutely necessary to..."

"Yes. Boats are small places. When someone releases their nasty attitude stink in an enclosed, shared space, someone's got to tell the offender to stop eating all those insecurity beans or go sit outside. Doug never mentioned any 'rules for good behavior' when he took us aboard. Brooding and judgment trips are bad form on a boat. Why shouldn't I called him on it?"

"Ah yes, Hanns, but we just lost our option to use the more productive tactic of putting up with his bullshit for two or three more days in the service of getting where we need to go. You may be right but you're not going to *fix* anything with this approach."

Voices and footsteps soon returned to the deck. "Here comes the inquisition."

Doug glowered with a plastic paddle in his hand, appearing more pathetic than threatening. Behind him stood two more men. Hanns could tell by their dress shirts they had just been recruited from the church. "I want you guys off my boat...NOW!"

Hanns appeared in the companionway and casually took a sip of his tea before responding. "I'll tell you what. Three of you might take the two of us but we're both in pretty good shape. My knife is sharp enough to hurt you if you even *look* at the blade from the wrong angle. The odds of you kicking me off this boat without getting seriously injured are nil. I don't know what the final outcome will be but I can promise you some serious trauma if anyone tries to physically remove me or Raquel. I won't go on the offensive but the first one to attack me might not see tomorrow.

"This is a simple contract dispute. Doug promised us passage to Puerto Rico. I'm holding him to his promise. Let's not turn a disagreement into a bloody brawl. I'm sorry you guys got pulled away from whatever you were doing but if a physical confrontation happens, you're starting the battle; I'll finish it. I'm not trespassing.

I haven't committed any crime. If you attack me and don't go to the hospital, you're going to jail—and threatening someone is assault; you're already over the legal line. Is this trip really necessary?"

The two men mumbled something in Doug's ear. Their body language clearly indicated they had no interest in participating in a brawl.

Hanns took another nonchalant sip of his tea.

The three men quietly returned to the dinghy and zoomed off toward shore.

"Somehow a trio of skinny guys with khaki slacks and Hawaiian ties didn't get my adrenaline going. The plastic dinghy paddle did add an element of comic relief; I had a hard time not laughing out loud. Not much of a fighting gang, are they?

"Can I interest you in another mattress dive before he comes back with the cavalry? After all, I thought I did a pretty good job with the whole alpha male routine and..."

"I hate when you make me laugh when I'm trying to be pissed off at you. No!"

"So what do you think is gonna happen next?"

"I'm not sure but we should get dressed and pack our stuff. I suspect 'psycho man' will decide he's not going to move the boat anywhere from here. He can't physically force us off but we can't force him to take the boat anywhere and I don't care to live with him while he waits us out."

"I don't think he's sophisticated enough to have stumbled across that option yet but you're right; a stalemate would not be pretty."

A half hour later, Doug returned once more with a uniformed man in a fiberglass motor launch.

After dismissing a long string of ridiculous, fabricated allegations, Hanns explained, "this is a simple matter. It's true we've had some differences of opinion with the captain of the vessel but he's been contracted to sail us to Isleta. We expect him to live up to his contract. We're carrying a lot of gear with us. Our goal is to get where we're going; we have no interest in staying here any longer than…"

"Air travel is already arranged. Put your bags on the launch. I'll take you to the airport. You'll be in Puerto Rico this afternoon. The tickets will cost you a hundred dollars but you'll be out of here. I'm sorry I can't do better than that."

Raquel responded before Hanns could open his mouth and get them more deeply entangled. "You're taking the last of our cash but if that gets us away from this psychotic nutcase, we'll jump on that plane"

Hanns took Doug's hand and shook it vigorously; he was too taken aback to protest. "Pleasure sailing with you, Doug."

Firing Squad

Luis Muñoz Marín Airport - San Juan, Puerto Rico

"Hanns, I'm glad to be off Doug's boat but I feel bad about the three people they dragged off the flight to make room for us and our luggage."

"I do too, but they're mostly inconvenienced. They'll call the boss and explain they'll be late to work on Monday. They get an extra day of vacation; they'll survive. If they didn't put us on that flight, we'd wind up spending the night in St. Maarten with all our shit; we've got way too little cash left to pay for taxis and hotels and all that. I don't know if Doug and his buddies or the St. Maarten Immigration Authority paid for our plane flight, but I'm sure our hundred dollars didn't cover the whole fare. I'm just happy as hell to be away from…"

Raquel reached into her bag. "Got your passport ready? I think we're next."

"Yeah." They stepped across the yellow line and handed their passports to a dark-haired man with a fine moustache.

"Ze purpose of your visit, *señor;* beesnees or pleasure?"

"Pleasure, sir, and my wife is American; she's coming home."

"Good. One moment sir." The man typed the passport numbers into a keyboard and stared into a screen. "Ees thees jour first time een Puerto Rico, Hanns?"

"No, sir. We've been through here many times."

"And where will jou be staying?"

"In Isleta for a few days, then on to Florida."

"I like Isleta. Ees a beautiful place. My brother-een-law, he like to veesit Isleta beddy much. Are jou a sailor?"

"Yes, sir."

"I haf always wanted to buy a boat and sail away. Eet sounds like a beddy eenteresting life."

"Yes, sir." Hanns smiled back. The man stared at his screen. Hanns raised an eyebrow at Raquel. Obviously, the customs agent was stalling. "Is there some sort of problem, sir? We can show other forms of identification if you want."

"Not at all, sir. Sometimes, de computer she run slow. Do you mind eef I take a look een your backpack, sir?"

"Not at all. Be my guest. There's a damp shirt and some swim shorts in there stuffed on top in a plastic bag. I can't promise they' smell too fresh but we ran out of time in St. Maarten and packed before everything dried." Hanns placed his backpack on a small steel table.

"Dat's alright, Hanns. Ees not a problem. Routine check."

"Open anything you want; I'm not hiding anything."

The agent poked through Hanns's backpack, lifting the flaps on pockets but not seriously inspecting their contents.

"Thees ees not my regular job. I work in de customs warehouse on de other side o' de airport but we had two people seeck today. Do you got any children, Hanns?"

"No, sir; no children."

"I haf t'ree. My oldes' son ees in ninth grade. I haf another who ees een fifth grade. I haf also a leettle girl t'ree years old."

Hanns nodded politely. *Why is this guy telling us his life story?*

Hanns studied the man halfheartedly rummaging through his backpack. Raquel tugged on his shirt; he scanned the room. The building now contained half as many people. The volume of ambient chatter subsided. An agent walked up to the people waiting in line behind them, "I'm sorry for your wait. Follow me to the other customs station in the next room; we'll get you taken care of."

Hanns whispered to Raquel, "do you see what I see?" The customs room continued to empty except for a dozen officers and a group of civilians talking with them. He shrugged at Raquel quizzically and put his hands on the table.

In a coordinated movement, everyone in the room turned to face them, drew pistols and shouted "FREEZE!" Officers and plain-clothed agents formed a semicircle around them.

Hanns raised his arms compliantly. A voice inside his head considered suggesting they'd formed their semicircle in such a way that the people at one end were at risk of being shot by the people at the other, but he thought better of trying to diffuse the situation with sarcasm. Raquel stared at him, hoping for an explanation. Hanns could only shrug.

The officers proceeded to tear their luggage apart, opening every bag and spreading the contents across several examination tables. "Please be careful with the small one, sir; that's my camera bag." Hanns stood quietly. He was allowed to lower his hands once he'd been thoroughly patted down. The agent said nothing. He began to open film canisters, shaking each of the rolls before recapping them. About halfway through the search, he spoke up. "Over here."

Two agents brought a film canister half-full of marijuana over to Hanns. "Surely this can't be the reason we're being detained? What's the fine for a quarter-ounce of old dope, anyway? If we had known we had any, we would have smoked it."

"Thees is not your beeg problem, sir. De fine is twainty dollars."

The man grabbed a receipt book, scribbled down "marijuana: less than ½ ounce: $20," tore off the sheet above the carbon paper and handed it to Hanns. He left the receipt book on the table. After the agent walked back to the luggage table, Hanns thumbed through the pages. "Raquel, check out how much contraband comes through this place in one day—marijuana, marijuana, cocaine, marijuana, quaaludes, marijuana, marijuana, quaaludes—it goes on and on. These goons made at least fifty drug seizures since this morning and that's only from people who got searched. Imagine how much shit walks right out the door."

Raquel rolled her eyes. "The bigger problem is we gave our last hundred bucks to the immigration man in St. Maarten. I have about six dollars left on me."

Hanns motioned for the agent to come back over. "Sir, I'm happy to pay the twenty dollar fine but if you check inside those wallets on the table, you'll see we're down to about ten dollars cash between us. We have money in the bank but we spent our last cash getting here to San Juan."

"Ees okay, sir. You can use a credit card."

"No cards, sir; we don't believe in them."

Hanns and Raquel followed the man to a small glass-walled office where they sat down in front of a steel desk. The man locked them in and left. "Who do we know in Puerto Rico who can help us with this mess?"

Raquel brightened, "how about Ramon Remos, the air-traffic controller? He and my sister became friends when she got sick right after you first met us, remember? He took care of her for several days. I think they're still in touch."

"Maybe. Let's try Ramon. Don't worry about the twenty bucks. If they can't squeeze the cash out of us, it'll cost them more to keep us in jail overnight and feed us. I'm more worried about the whole firing squad fiasco. What the hell was that about?"

Raquel got up and stepped behind the desk. "Hmmm, it says here on the screen you're an international terrorist, a drug-smuggler, a gun runner, a money launderer, and wow, sweetie, I'm just so happy to know you're not a pedophile...though there's a second page I don't know how to get to on this computer. Any laws you haven't broken, yet? Is there any substance to any of this?"

"Raquel, I promise you I have absolutely no fucking idea what this is about. I've been involved in my share of mischief in my life, but I never stole anything or got involved with drugs or guns or crime. You've seen me deal with plenty of assholes; I never hurt or killed even the ones who deserved it."

"Okay. Sorry, but I had to ask. If this is all some strange mistake, I'm with you. As long as you're telling the truth, I'll help you through. We'll figure out what..."

An agent gave them a cold stare through the glass. They stepped away from the flickering green letters on the tiny monitor.

Raquel found Ramon's number in her purse and got a nod of assent to use the phone. She dialed and got no answer.

An hour later, she was able to explain their predicament to Ramon.

For another hour, Hanns and Raquel sat waiting in silence, watching passengers filter through the customs stations through the glass walls of the surrounding offices.

Ramon arrived.

"Raquel, dig the body language. I don't think our friend Ramon is an air-traffic controller." The customs agents stiffened and greeted him with respect as he entered. "They're treating him like he's a superior; they're practically standing at attention."

Ramon spoke with the agents for a moment, walked into the office and sat down at the desk.

"Hello, Hanns. Hello, Raquel. Quite a mess you're in."

"Thanks for coming, Ramon, we've been…"

"Tell me…" Ramon leaned across the desk, passed a folder to Hanns and looked him straight in the eye. "…ees der any substance to *any* of thees? Do jou know anytheeng about *anytheeng* here? Gimme straight talk, Hanns—no games."

Hanns scanned the pages in the file. "Ramon, I promise you I have absolutely no clue what's going on here."

"Jou are serious?"

"No idea. If I had a rap sheet like that, I wouldn't jump off an invisible sailboat, fly into an international airport and hand my passport to the authorities. Anyone with a record like this would be slick enough to keep sailing and lurk in the shadows, don't you think?"

Ramon stood up. "Wait here a minute. I get jou out of thees."

"Who are you, Ramon? I don't think you're an air traffic controller."

"Wait here a minute," Ramon said tersely. "I be right back."

Ramon walked out, spoke with a few people and then returned.

"Jou are released eento my custody. Jou can stay weeth me for a few days. I take jou back to Isleta to get jour stuff out of storage tomorrow."

Invicta
Melbourne, Florida–February 1980

In Xanadu did Kubla Khan
A stately pleasure-dome decree.

"The lines are beautiful. Tell me about her, Mr. North."

North's expression displayed the affected disinterest of a seller who had already resolved to part with a prized possession at first, but as he began to speak, a certain prideful glow spread across his features. "Are you familiar with William H. Tripp, the yacht designer?"

"Sure; he did the Hinckley Bermuda 40, the Mercer 44, the Pearson Invicta, the Tripp 30, the Block Island 40 and some designs for Catalina that look like giant floating duck's heads to me. I don't care for the Catalina's unprotected rudders and fin keels, but his full-keel boats have lines I believe were inspired by some of the graceful old John Alden boats. He died at the top of his game in a traffic accident, didn't he?"

"Yes, in 1971." North closed his eyes. "He was a good friend of mine. Back in '58, he showed me the lines of the Invicta while he was still working on them. The drawings wowed me; I told him

I'd be his first customer. As it turns out, he was designing the boat for the first customer so I became the second customer and ordered hull number two. The mold was built by Palmer Johnson in Sturgeon Bay, Wisconsin, but I don't think the right to manufacture the Invicta design was officially spoken for by anyone at the time; I believe he only contracted Palmer to build the mold. We started the layup at Palmer Johnson and finished the deck and hull there before Pearson Yachts bought the design. She ended up getting shipped to the Pearson yard in Bristol, Rhode Island where they finished the interior and the rig. Back in 1959, fiberglass was a new material for boat-building; polyester resin was even newer. I didn't trust the new resins so I had 200 gallons of 2:1 epoxy shipped over from Europe to Palmer Johnson. That hull you're looking at is one-inch-thick, solid epoxy glass; there isn't a stronger boat in the world not made from steel of the same thickness."

Hanns climbed the ladder leaning against the hull where the yawl sat propped up in the boatyard, her bottom already pressure-washed to receive a new coat of paint. He sketched a rough picture of a yawl on a yellow pad and made small notes with arrows pointing to various parts of the illustrated vessel. *Get rid of this mizzen mast. Reinforce the foredeck and add more cleats.* Down below he continued his survey. *An alcohol stove? They're science's best attempt yet at light without heat.* He imagined tearing everything apart and starting over, but what a fantastic place to start from. There was no better-built, better-designed or better-sailing hull than this. Hanns opened the engine hatch and examined the gasoline-powered Atomic four-cylinder engine. He measured the engine compartment and went through a small catalog of diesel engines in his mind. *If I customize the engine mounts, I bet I can wedge a Volvo diesel in here.*

North climbed up the ladder to continue speaking with Hanns from the cockpit over the bridge deck. "What did you sail before?"

"I had a Sparkman and Stephens 57—a great cruising boat but with old wooden boats you spend as much time working on them as sailing. I got rid of her in the South Pacific and bought a 47-foot trimaran which I took all over the Caribbean. Multihulls are incredible machines; they're fast, shallow-draft and roomy but they're high-performance boats. The stresses on them, especially on the bridges between the hulls are immense. They make for level, comfortable sailing but they get driven hard. They can fly more canvas than a comparable monohull so everything on those boats gets double the abuse. Lines part. Sheaves break. They're fantastic cruising machines but I'm an engineer; I'm constantly calculating the stresses on the various parts of the boat and I'm ready for a vessel that doesn't inspire so much mathematical backchatter in my mind when the wind and seas pick up. A good monohull is nowhere near as fast but when stresses exceed a certain level, it heels and spills the wind. I intend to start with a first-rate cruising monohull and design a compact, comfortable, luxurious living space inside."

"You've done some sailing. Good. Have you ever been out on a boat when the seas start to pick up? Maybe you've put a reef or two in the sails? You're honking along at hull speed and you know there's some real shit coming but when you watch how the boat moves with the waves, you can tell she's having fun? Many boats are designed to be comfortable coastal cruisers; few are real passage-makers. Get out in blue water with this boat; you'll know Bill Tripp was an experienced offshore sailor who paid attention to how a hull interacts with the waves. He designed her to be safe, balanced and stable in a big sea. She may be nothing but a hunk of fiberglass but get her in the ocean; I swear you'll hear her laughing."

Hanns sat down in the main saloon. She was a narrow boat, built more to carry a team of seven on ocean races than to provide a habitat for two people with occasional guests, but the space had wonderful possibilities. Most monohulls had squarish cabin trunks extending above a ring of deck; the Invicta's bubble-shaped cabin provided ample room below and more useful deck space above for handling sails and living life. Behind the foredeck, a large hatch opened facing aft, allowing air to be drawn in through the companionway while preventing spray from entering. Hanns lay on the settee staring up at the bubble with its two small bronze ports.

"I'll take her."

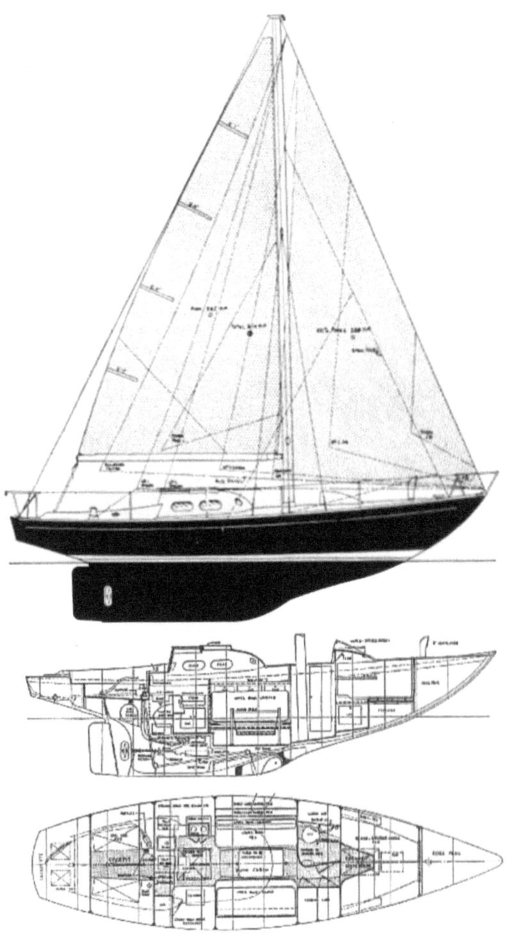

THE INVICTA

The Seventh Chakra

Melbourne, Florida–July, 1980

"Okay, Raquel. Open your eyes."

"Hanns, she's beautiful. I love the nameplate on the transom. What does *Seventh Chakra* mean?"

"Hindu medicine describes seven *chakras* or energy centers; they correspond to different parts of the body rising up through the spine to the top of the head. Each energy center relates to specific body functions and also to various instincts and forms of emotional expression. The seventh *chakra* is *Sahasrara;* it symbolizes inner wisdom and the death of our bodies, kharma and the idea that mental and physical actions are all part of a universal chain of interconnected consciousness."

"You surprise me sometimes."

"Well, I'm not so religious as I am philosophical. The titles we live under exert some sort of psychological influence on our lives. *Windship Chaos* was a wonderful ship. I had some of the great times of my life aboard her, but I had my share of chaos aboard her, too. Maybe this is catalyzed by the fact I'll be turning forty next week but I don't see myself as a young man blasting my way across the oceans any more. Rest assured I haven't lost my taste for fun but I sailed thousands of miles, crossed oceans, weathered storms, slept with plenty of women and did all the things a young man might need to do to prove himself to himself. I'm proud of my chaotic existence; I jumped out of the mainstream and drank from the cup of life in a way few people ever give themselves a chance to but now, if I'm going to keep sailing, I need to change the pace, slow down and smell the roses a bit, stay in some of those anchorages a while longer. We started to do that in Dominica; that was the first time in many years I enjoyed having a stationary home base.

"*Windship Chaos* was built for fast, efficient traveling. *The Seventh Chakra* is an ocean-going travel machine but philosophically, she's not about traveling so much as conscious living and being and expression. You won't find a galley like this on a boat twice her size. The main saloon is all about open space and comfort. I installed a pull-out screen for showing my slides. I put in a dive compressor so I can fill my tanks on board. This boat is as capable of circumnavigating the planet as *Windship Chaos,* but sailing *around* the world is quite different from sailing *in* the world. I'm ready to take my time and just be. The name *Seventh Chakra* is a reminder to focus on wisdom, life and death, the interconnectedness of all things and personal evolution.

"Together, you and I can…"

"Well, Hanns, I don't know how to tell you this, but you know how I'm always so fatigued lately? Lots of flu symptoms? So many aches and pains? I went to the doctor this morning and…"

"And what?"

"Leukemia. The prognosis is not good. Philosophically, you and I have arrived at the same place. I love you dearly but I'm afraid we must part. Too soon, my love, it will be time for you to sail on without me."

Opportunity Knocks

Nassau Harbour, Bahamas – October, 1980

Nassau was the usual zoo but Hanns paid little attention. Sure, the harbour was noisy and congested but anchoring here meant easy access to supplies. Mostly, New Providence was away from Florida and friends left behind. The beautiful Bahamian wilderness lay a half-day's sail beyond Nassau's back door but why hurry? Much remained to be done on the boat. Canvas awnings and covers needed to be sewn. Parts required welding or fabrication on a small machinist's lathe. Better not to run out of epoxy or break a tool anchored in some remote place where replacing it would not be an option. Cruising would come soon enough. Hanns put his engineer's hat over his philosopher's cap and patiently transformed *Seventh Chakra* into a place of comfort, style and efficient living. Four speakers and a good hi-fi system drowned out much of the external, surrounding noise from the harbour along with emotional noise from within.

Nevertheless, Hanns heard the sound of the other boat. The noise of a diesel resonated through his hull as the yacht passed by within inches. "Goddamned idiot!" He sprang to the cockpit. "What the hell is wrong with you?"

This was the third day in a row the *Wild Cherry* had barreled by way too close. Hanns had had enough. By the time the fifty-six foot schooner tied to the dock to disgorge its flock of sunburned tourists, he was waiting with clenched fists, ready to knock the helmsman in the water. "Who's the Captain of this vessel?"

"Dot would be me, suh. Jus' a minnit." A large black man with a striped tank top and mirrored sunglasses shot Hanns an uncomprehending grin.

"Who taught you to operate a boat? What kind of idiot..."

A thin, dark gentleman with a beige sport jacket and a Panama hat stepped in front of Hanns and extended a hand. "I'm afraid we haven't met yet. My name is James Darling. How can I help you?"

"Do you have anything to do with the *Wild Cherry?*"

"I'm the owner, but my crew runs the charters for me. What seems to be the trouble?"

Hanns explained his concerns about the *Wild Cherry's* daily, intentional near-collisions.

Darling smiled. "Rocky's a no-brainer. I'll take care of this.

"Rocky, this man is a friend of mine. Come anywhere near his boat again, you'll be selling postcards at the straw market. Got me?"

"Yes, boss."

"Rocky's alright; no rocket surgeon, but a good sailor. He's a young man feelin' full of himself because he's in command of a big, fancy boat full of hot young tourist girls. He tries to show off in stupid ways; he's still green. After he's been doin' this a few months, the novelty will wear off; bein' captain will be just another job.

"As soon as you do something for a livin'," Darling continued in his pleasant Bahamian burr, "even if it's the most enjoyable thing in the world, the fact that you *have* to do it quickly outweighs the luxury of knowin' you can do it any time you want. So many fine yachts sit in this marina for months or years at a time. Their owners pay for the ability to exercise the option to sail in the Bahamas whenever they like...and that's precisely why they don't actually do it. The dream is more pleasant than the reality. That ketch over there on the next pier has had a crew keeping her varnish up and scrubbing the mildew out of her cabin for five years; I've never seen her leave the dock." Darling laughed.

Hanns warmed to his host quickly. "So many people chase the cruising dream. They retire and buy a comfortable yacht but they never imagine the storms and the reefs and the mosquitoes and the varnish work. I don't know what these people are thinking but I see them get disillusioned. Paradise is beautiful but it can be a scary place where it takes hard work and quick wits to survive. You can blast into New Providence on a cruise ship and do nothing but eat and drink for a week but that's a lot different than diving for your dinner, keeping your diesel running, trimming the sails and steering a compass course."

"Hanns, I grew up here in Nassau goin' to church every Sunday." Darling took off his jacket and slung it over his shoulder. "I wonder how many people think heaven will be like a big cruise ship where they sit around the pool gettin' drunk while waiters and porters attend to all their needs. Does a staff of poor immigrants take care of the chosen people in the promised land, or is heaven a place where we experience the joy of self-reliance?"

"I'm not a religious man, James, but I've had more than my fair share of times when I thought I was about to find out whether or not I should have been. I never worried about whether I was going to heaven or hell but the one thing that always ran across my mind when I thought I was going to die was, 'Not now. I'm having way too much fun.'"

"So, you're neither an ordinary tourist nor an ordinary yachtsman," observed Darling. "What brings you to a place like Nassau?"

"A compromise—I'm a boat builder, a metal fabricator and an engineer. I'm finishing up my vision of the ultimate cruising boat. My wife passed away not long ago; I wanted to get away and start over. Once I got the engine installed and most of the important projects done, I figured I'd get to the details in the islands."

"I'm sorry."

"Thank you but we had incredible times together—no regrets—nothing left unsaid. She was a great friend. Losing Raquel is a deep loss, but I'm moving on. I'm okay with it.

"If you're interested, I'd be happy to show you the boat."

"Let's do that tomorrow evening. I'd love to take the tour. Are you doing your own engine work?"

"I do *all* my own work; diesel, electrical, plumbing, sail repair, canvas, welding and fabricating; I have ridiculously high standards. Most commercial operations don't deliver the polish I insist on. I don't mean to come off as a braggart, but..."

"I could use a capable bosun aboard the *Wild Cherry.* When you're runnin' charters, it's important to keep the engine workin', the sails trimmed and the passengers babysat. Rocky's a good helmsman when he's not playin' kid games but if somethin' needs to be fixed, he's useless. I'd love to have someone aboard who knows how to correct or bypass a problem without panickin' anyone. Have you ever been adrift with a boatload of tourists?"

"No thanks on drifting with tourists, but I could use the work."

"Next cruise is our Sunset Special. We leave again in about an hour. Why don't you come with us?"

"Maybe I will. Thanks for being so professional about everything. I'm afraid I got my temper up and..."

"I'm sorry about Rocky runnin' you down but that's under control from now on. I'm glad his mischief brought you here to my dock, though; I'm happy to meet you. I'll look forward to havin' some capable crew aboard and to checkin' out your boat."

Darling introduced Hanns to Rocky who responded like a big, friendly dog and then to the two other crew members. "Hanns will be our new bosun on the *Wild Cherry.* He can fix anythin' and he's an experienced sailor and navigator. Treat him with respec', boys.

"And one more thing, Hanns...," Darling smiled conspiratorialy.

"What's that?"

"Wait here for a moment; I'll be right back."

Darling walked down to the beginning of the pier, reaching the office just as the marina manager was exiting. After exchanging words and greetings, they went back inside together.

On the dock, Hanns familiarized himself with the rigging of the *Wild Cherry,* studying her lines and calculating how her ketch rig would behave on different points of sail.

Darling returned with a small brown envelope. "This is a gift to apologize for Rocky playing chicken with you and to welcome you aboard my crew. Don't open the package 'til you get home."

Diesel Doc

Nassau Harbor, Bahamas–October, 1980

Even in this poor country where skilled workers were needed, the locals could be litigious about foreigners "taking their jobs away;" a Bahamian work permit was a key to the islands. For Hanns, the paper meant no more sneaking around the docks—no more worrying whether clients would find it cheaper to report him to the immigration authorities than to pay him for his work.

Afternoon and evening sails aboard the *Wild Cherry* became a pleasant enough way to earn a living. During the slower summer months, Hanns updated her rigging, changing her aging stays and shrouds one at a time, and splicing up new wire-to-rope halyards. Under his tutelage, her crew brought her teak rails and hatches back up to snuff. Hanns showed them his trick of adding a pinch of gold metallic powder to the varnish to make the finish appear thicker, and set up a schedule for maintaining it section-by-section.

Moreover, working on a well-kept boat on the Nassau docks was the best advertising imaginable. Hanns had a local vendor make up a few-dozen white polo shirts with DIESEL DOC • QUALITY MARINE SERVICES emblazoned across the backs. A second set of bright yellow shirts featured an image of a cherry on their pockets above the word CREW. Rocky and the rest of Darling's boys wore one shirt or the other depending on whether the ship was under weigh or at the dock. Darling was happy to see his yacht tight and tidy. Hanns, looking like he had a half-dozen men in his employ, was approached almost daily by transient yachtsmen needing repairs and upgrades.

As the hot, slow days of summer yielded to the busy tourist season, the *Seventh Chakra* came together, too. With an ample supply of money, sailing and tourist girls, life was good, even in Nassau's commercial harbour.

By late October, winter cold fronts often made the weather too windy, rainy or rough to sail the *Wild Cherry*. Hanns divided his time between his own boat and well-paying jobs on the docks.

Today's weather was especially nasty and expected to remain so. Secure in a slip in the marina, Hanns hardly felt the storm. He used the time to run wires from *The Seventh Chakra's* forward cabin back to a new circuit breaker panel. Fans and stereo speakers made the forward berth more comfortable.

But in the big seas north of New Providence, life afloat held less appeal. Marco Jimenez and his wife Carmen, only a few days out from Florida on *Fool's Gold,* their 48-foot Hatteras motor yacht, had never experienced seas like this before. Running south from the Berry Islands to Nassau in enormous swells, Marco worked the throttle levers on his two big diesels, trying to move at the same speed as the waves so as not be overtaken or dive forward into the troughs. A turn back to port against wind and seas was not a safe option. Carmen took to her bunk an hour out of Chub Cay where she lay moaning, too seasick to be scared.

Marco drove toward New Providence. A pouring rain obscured all visibility. Inexperienced and scared, he gave up on finding Nassau's well-marked harbour and instead, pushed generally south with the swells, passing across the reef line through a narrow cut between two long strips of coral under the divine protection afforded to drunks, nincompoops, inexperienced mariners and the extraordinarily lucky. Anchored in shallow water behind a tiny islet over which the waves broke explosively, *Fool's Gold* pitched and rolled through the night. Marco prayed to God, the saints, various angels and other deities contrived for the occasion for his anchors to hold.

Hold they did, but with her engines shut down, wallowing in the seas, the yacht's two eight-inch exhaust ports submerged repeatedly, then lifted high into the air as her bow pitched forward. Gallons of water poured through the exhaust pipes, up into the engine manifolds, through the open valves and into the cylinders.

In the morning, after the front had blown through, Marco was surprised how cold it was but delighted to find the seas calmed and the water cleared. Carmen's greenish hue faded. Nassau Harbour should be an easy run from here. Already, the impossible blue clarity of the Bahamian shallows began to eclipse the memory of last night's ordeal.

Marco turned the two ignition keys halfway, one with each hand. He listened for a few seconds to the squealing of the horns indicating the engine preheaters were working. Turning the keys all the way to the right, he engaged two high-torque starter motors which in-turn, engaged two massive flywheels. The effect of this on the two water-filled diesels was catastrophic. With a profound *clunk,* valves and piston rods, unable to compress the water in the cylinders, assumed a variety of C and S-shaped configurations—rendering them unfit for further service as anything other than abstract sculpture.

As the towboat approached the dock, Hanns and Marco spotted one another—a match made in heaven.

Hanns shook Marco's hand. "Water in both engines, eh?"

Marco's expression was incredulous. "Why do you think I have...?"

"You have two engines out. You're not wrecked out on the reef or up on the shore. I figure you anchored out in that shit we had last night, scooped up water with those big exhausts of yours and flooded your engines before trying to start them. If I'm right, both engines need to be rebuilt. I can do it for you, but I have other projects going, too and we'll need to order parts. I'll need four-to-six weeks to get them both done."

Marco stared at his feet pensively. "The towing company wants $20,000 to send a boat big enough to tow me back to Miami. On the radio, the man at Nassau Diesel said the same thing about having water in the cylinders but he told me nobody on the island can do the job; it requires some sort of special equipment."

"Usually, it does," affirmed Hanns, "but here in the islands, we improvise. To rebuild those engines, you need a lift to raise them up so you can drop the crank and pistons out the bottom. You're right; the engine hoisting equipment doesn't exist here—and Nassau Diesel has plenty of much easier jobs lined up—but there are other ways to lift heavy objects. I can do the job for half the towing cost."

"$10,000! What about doing only one of the engines? Then I can motor back and..."

"You don't really want to risk getting caught out in conditions like you saw last night with one untested engine, do you?"

Carmen threw Marco a frosty glance, effectively retiring the question.

The towboat delivered *Fool's Gold* to a slip in the marina one pier over from the *Seventh Chakra.* Marco took up residence at the dock to supervise the repairs. Carmen flew home to Miami.

The next day, Hanns appeared with a dock cart loaded with two-by-four boards. He stacked the lumber neatly on the finger pier adjacent to *Fool's Gold's* deck. A second cartload brought four small, hydraulic automotive jacks.

After unbolting the port engine from its mounts, Hanns disconnected the exhaust system and jacked one side high enough to insert a piece of lumber under the block. Repeating the process with the other side, board-by-board, he slowly raised the diesel up off its bed—high enough to drop the oil pan, access the inside of the engine and with some uncomfortable contortions, work beneath it for short intervals.

The jacking-up process took two days, after which good weather made afternoon and evening sails aboard the *Wild Cherry* Hanns's priority.

Marco ordered parts from the States and waited for a piston kit and a gasket kit. After they arrived, he placed an additional order for essential gaskets not included with the gasket kit, tools and manuals. Each shipment took over a week to arrive. Import duties doubled the costs. After three weeks, he grew impatient.

James Darling came down the pier to the *Wild Cherry* and put an arm around Hanns's shoulder. "How you doin', my boy? How things goin' with your big diesel job?"

Hanns laughed. "Marco came up to me this morning all full of smiles, telling me the 'good news;' he's going to get me some 'help.'"

"That boy's cheap as they come. Watch yourself. I've seen yachtsmen jus' like him many times on these docks. If you…"

"I have his number. I smile and play his game," Hanns assured. "I'm better at the game than he is. He just doesn't know it."

Miguel came recommended by a friend of Carmen's brother. Though he lacked experience working on diesels, he'd been a service station mechanic for years; he knew what to do with a ratchet wrench. A paid trip to stay on a yacht in the Bahamas sounded like the opportunity of a lifetime. He'd accrued some vacation days and readily took Marco up on his offer. Miguel's first mistake: arriving in Nassau airport with a blue mechanic's shirt on and a heavy bag of tools. His second mistake: explaining to the customs official that the purpose of his visit was to work on a boat in the marina.

The customs agent grinned, confiscated his tools, shook his head and promised he could pick them up on his way back of the country.

Relegated to light duty as Hanns's assistant, Miguel spent work-days handing wrenches and screwdrivers and parts to Hanns under the engine. "You realize," explained Hanns to Marco, "I can't guarantee the work if someone else does the job."

On days when the *Wild Cherry* demanded Hanns's attention, Marco begged Miguel to borrow Hanns's tools but as a mechanic himself, he knew better than to ask. Marco almost came to blows with him over his refusal. Miguel spent his idle days exploring Fort Charlotte, the Straw Market and the Queen's Staircase. After a week, he flew home, his contrived excuse to Marco—customs had only granted him a seven-day stay. Miguel accomplished little on the engines. He found a 'renegotiated' fee in his envelope when he returned to Florida.

After five weeks, Hanns finished removing the boards and bolting the first engine back down onto its original bed. After reconnecting the exhaust, fuel system and electrical components, he twisted the key. The diesel turned over a few times and sprang to life. He let the machine come to temperature, listened and made a few adjustments.

"How far behind is Marco in paying you?" asked Darling. "He owes the marina a month's rent."

"He's into me about three thousand dollars."

Darling looked concerned. "That boy's gonna run out on you, now he got a workin' engine. I'll bet you anything."

Hanns smiled and flashed his eyebrows. "I warned him I still had critical adjustments to make. He promised me he wouldn't run the engine under any circumstances."

"You think he's gonna listen?"

"Not my problem."

Another cold front blew through and continued south, bringing cool temperatures and light wind in its wake. Hanns had the *Seventh Chakra's* hatches shut tight to keep warm below. He slept under two extra blankets. But even with his boat closed up, he heard the diesel start at two in the morning. The engine revved higher and higher, accelerating out of control. Without opening his eyes, he counted forty-seven seconds before the runaway engine, spinning much faster than it was ever designed to, stopped abruptly with an oddly musical, bell-like clang that hung over the still, crisp air of the otherwise quiet harbour.

Hanns inhaled deeply, sighed, adjusted his blankets and drifted back to sleep.

The morning was especially cold: nearly 50°F. Hanns found no reason to venture outside until well after sunup and a mug of steaming hot tea. After sleeping in, Hanns put his sea jacket on over a wool sweater and ventured out. He met Marco carrying a duffel bag down the pier in the other direction.

"Laundry?" asked Hanns, looking at Marco's bag cynically.

"Some mechanic you are. I…"

"You tried to run the engine, didn't you, Marco?"

"I wanted to test it. It was so good to hear the motor running yesterday and I…"

"At two in the morning? Didn't you promise not to touch it?"

"Yeah, but all I did was…"

"All you did was blow up a perfectly good engine. If you hadn't fucked around with it, everything would have been fine. You tried to run off on me last night. Call a tugboat if you want your engines fixed. I'm done with you…and I intend to be paid for the last three weeks of lying on my back in your goddamned bilge with a wrench in my hand."

Marco looked around as if some avenue of escape might somehow present itself on the long, narrow pier where Hanns stood between him and the gate. "Look. I'm sorry. I'll have the money next week. I'm waiting on a check and I'll..."

Hanns stood his ground.

When Marco reached the gate, he had parted with his gold Rolex watch, his two gold rings and his heavy gold chain.

Six weeks later, a representative from an American bank arrived to assess the condition of *Fool's Gold* and pay off the lien put on her by the marina.

The towboat arrived a week later.

"I told you Marco was gonna run off on you, Hanns," admonished Darling.

"And I told you it would be his problem if he did." Hanns reached into his pocket, extracted a small metal object and pressed the fuel governor pin from Marco's diesel into Darling's palm.

Wild Dolphins

Nassau Harbor, Bahamas–January, 1981

A tentative voice called to the *Wild Cherry* from the dock. "Excuse me. I know I'm early, but I have tickets for the evening sail. Do you mind if I come aboard now?"

Hanns looked down from the deck on a tall young woman wearing a rather ridiculous, oversized sun hat and a long, blue cotton dress. Thin and attractive in an unglamorous, unpretentious way, she had a genuine smile Hanns found appealing.

Darling winked at Hanns. "Why don't you entertain our guest while the crew makes ready for the cruise?"

Hanns extended a hand to the gangplank. "Welcome to the *Wild Cherry*. I'm Hanns."

"Carla." The woman walked quite comfortably across the narrow gangplank but took his hand anyway. "Carla Marla."

"Fantastic name."

"I was going to change my name to Carla Schmarla so nobody would believe me or know what to say when they were fed up with me but I never got around to it." She giggled at her own joke.

Hanns laughed with her. "How long will you be here in Nassau?"

"Not long at this rate. I'm about done with t-shirt hawkers, casinos and steel bands…and the captive dolphins doing stupid tricks over on Paradise Island make my blood boil. I just walked out of one of their dog and pony dolphin shows and…"

"I agree with you," said Hanns. "I've been observing dolphins in the wild for many years. They're smart, social, and by the way, one of the few animals beside humans that engages in sex for pleasure. That, alone, makes them advanced in my book."

"I guess it does," Carla giggled again. "How do you observe dolphins in the wild?"

"See the boat tied up over there? She's my home. I've been all over this planet and encountered dolphins everywhere. There's even a species of pink dolphin living in the Amazon River. Dolphins play in my bow wake all the time. Look one in the eye and you'll immediately appreciate its high level of comprehension and intelligence. To enclose an animal that roams hundreds of miles every day in a tiny tank is criminal; I agree with you."

"Well," returned Carla, grateful to find someone whose interests ranged beyond commerce, "I somehow pictured the Bahamas as a wilder and frankly freer place. I did get out on a pleasant-enough SCUBA excursion but the rest of this trip has mostly consisted of wandering around, dodging people selling stuff and watching the whores and gamblers in the casinos. Now, there's a scene that will make you cynical about…"

"So, you're jaded with humanity and also a SCUBA diver? If you're up for adventure, stay sober tonight on the *Wild Cherry* cruise and don't overeat. I've got SCUBA gear on my boat and an idea in my head. Your vacation to Tinseltown just took a turn for the better."

After a noisy and uneventful sail on the too-crowded *Wild Cherry,* Carla was hesitant to risk any more of her evening on Hanns but ultimately decided to follow him down the dock to the *Seventh Chakra* where he revealed his plan.

"Come on. The moon is full; we'll be able to see without electric lights and the wind is almost completely calm."

She looked at him with a half smile. "You're serious aren't you?"

"Yeah. Put this wetsuit on. We'll be black—invisible. We'll arrive about two in the morning, get the job done and be back in the dinghy in a half-hour."

"What if we're caught?"

"If we get caught, we'll drop the tools and they'll kick us out. Swimming is no crime and trespassing is likely to be treated as a nuisance. Tourists misbehave every day. Who did you say you worked for, again?"

"The U.S. Department of Energy. You know, the people who brought you Hiroshima and Nagasaki?"

"I don't think the Bahamian hotel staff wants to mess with Uncle Sam. They'll give you a spanking and make you stand with your nose in a corner."

"This is just crazy enough to work. Fuck it; I'm going to make this a vacation to remember. Let's do this!"

"There's the spirit."

Hanns got into the dinghy first, then helped Carla climb down from the stern of the *Seventh Chakra.* He untied the painter[19] and started the engine. They idled out of the marina, picking up speed after distancing themselves from the sleeping boats.

Hanns spoke into her ear over the noise of the outboard motor. "Getting around Paradise Island to the outside is about a four mile trip. We'll look for a place to anchor the dinghy where it's out of sight and out of reach."

For twenty-five minutes, they motored wordlessly out of the harbor, beyond the lights of Nassau and around a narrow spit of dark, undeveloped land surrounded by mangroves and covered with scrub jungle. Outside the harbour in the ocean, waves rolled gently toward a white, sandy beach glowing in the moonlight.

Hanns brought the engine to idle. "I'm going to anchor a little farther out than I originally planned, beyond the line of surf; the white sand bottom here makes us more visible than I'd like. We'll have to swim a bit farther to get to shore, but the dinghy will be better hidden over these seagrass beds and small coral heads. See the radio tower?"

19 a dinghy's bow line is called a *painter.*

"Yes."

"The tower lines up with the corner of the hotel in front of it."

"Uh-huh."

"That line is our bearing. On the far end of the island, notice another building with a construction site in front of it. Find some part of each structure to line up. When we swim out, we'll be able to find our way back to the dinghy by lining up our two ranges."

"You've done this before, haven't you?"

Hanns smiled, put on his mask, put his regulator in his mouth, took a breath and flipped backward off the inflated pontoon of the dinghy into the warm, clear water. Carla splashed in behind him.

Carla motioned for him to come up and took her regulator out of her mouth. "I thought night diving was going to be dark and creepy. This is beautiful, almost like swimming in daylight."

"Surprising, isn't it? The water is clear and the moonlight is powerful. Let's snorkel in to shore to save some air. Once we're inside, breathe long and slow so your bubbles don't make an obvious disturbance."

She nodded. They continued their way through the surf up into a narrow channel entrance.

Hanns signaled to switch from snorkel to scuba. They submerged, keeping close to the bottom of a series of connected lagoons. The water was dark and greener here—not very pleasant—but the lights on the hotel grounds made it easy to find their way while adding a cover of rippling reflection on the surface.

Under a small foot bridge, Hanns stood up in neck-deep water. He took out his regulator, flipped his face mask up on top of his head and whispered. "This is perfect. I think they designed this gate to make things convenient for us. The bridge will give us the cover we need and…." He held his finger to his lips; a chattering couple walk over the boards above them.

Carla giggled mischievously.

"Keep your head above the surface. Kick me if anything happens I need to know about."

She nodded. Hanns replaced his regulator and descended.

The gate was made from galvanized fencing like one might find around a typical baseball field. Though thickly covered with marine growth, it yielded wire-by-wire to Hanns's bolt-cutters. Hanns waved a hand in front of his face. Green sparks of phosphorescence danced through his fingers. He continued to cut at the wire. A gray form flashed by on the other side of the fence. After ten minutes of cutting, Hanns pulled a two-foot diameter circle of fencing out of the gate and returned to the surface.

Carla put a finger to her lips and aimed her thumb up at the bridge. Someone was standing above their heads.

Hanns nodded and waited. He took Carla's hand.

A large, gray mass shot by them, glowing green, moving gracefully through the phosphorescent water. Whoever was on the bridge didn't react.

Hanns suppressed a snicker.

A second dolphin swam for freedom. Carla and Hanns remained still and quiet. Still no motion on the bridge.

The third and fourth animals made their breaks. A whistle blew. A shout rang out. Footsteps above them ran off.

"Let's go!"

Skimming the bottom, they swam as fast as they could through the small marina where the hotel kept its fleet of watercraft and continued out the channel. Hanns located the dinghy easily. They climbed in, gasping from exertion and laughing. Hanns pulled the anchor aboard and almost yanked the starter cord before thinking better of it. Free of his bulky SCUBA tank but still wearing his fins, he dived in once more to tow the boat a few hundred yards farther out of earshot before starting the motor and zooming back to the marina.

Carla beamed. "I never had so much fun in my life."

"Me neither! Those assholes pay hundreds of thousands of dollars for wild dolphins. This ought to put a kink in their hoses."

"There are some happy dolphins in the Atlantic tonight."

"Yes," laughed Hanns, "and they're probably miles away by now; they're not stupid."

"Well, my Nassau vacation certainly turned around. The first thing I'm going to do is take you home to your place. I hope you don't think I'm being forward?"

"Not at all. I must confess I was going to angle in that direction, anyway. . .and the second thing?"

"I've been working for the DOE for a long time. The job isn't particularly bad but I'm realizing the last ten years haven't been particularly *anything.* What we just did feels like living. I'm not wealthy by any means but I have a small inheritance sitting in the bank waiting for 'some day.' Well, 'some day' is today. In the morning, if you'll accept a stowaway, I'm going to call my boss and tell him I won't be returning to work. If our paths diverge in a week, that will be part of my adventure but if you never choose a day, 'some day' is a destructive fabrication. My focus in life just shifted to *now.*"

Hanns twisted the throttle. The dinghy climbed up on a plane, skimming around the point back into New Providence Harbour toward where the *Seventh Chakra* lay waiting in her slip.

Greeting Committee
August, 1981–Eight Months Later

A windless afternoon; the waters of the Gulf Stream undulated slowly—placid, sheets of cobalt glass a hundred feet long and six inches high. For a short time that morning off Bimini, the Gulf Stream Spotted Dolphins came by to play in the *Seventh Chakra's* bow wake. Mostly, the day had been long hours of motoring and hiding from the sun under the cockpit awning. Useless, the sails were furled but the auto-pilot kept a straight course without complaint. Now, the skyline of West Palm Beach sat atop the horizon. Hanns spoke over the thrum of the diesel, "breaking out of earth orbit is hard enough to accomplish but coming back is the tough part. The sailing lifestyle and the island settings change you at a core level. You'll feel it the first time you go into a crowded grocery store or hear angry drivers honk their horns in traffic."

"Maybe so, but since I made the spontaneous decision to quit a pretty good government job and blast off into outer space, I accumulated a lot of loose ends and people who think I'm crazy. To slowly let go of your attachments is one thing. Wishing everyone well and splitting, telling my best friend she has a new cat and making lease payments on a car that sits rusting in my parents' driveway are other things altogether. I don't want to go back any more than you do, but sailing will be much more fun after I put my abandoned past in order. We won't need to be here long."

Hanns glanced at the engine temperature gauge. "I'm bracing myself for the adjustment. I'm picking up the 'city vibe' as Palm Beach gets closer. We should be inside in less than two hours."

"I know, but I am looking forward to introducing you to my parents; it's a chick thing."

Hanns chuckled. "Glass of tea?"

"Sure."

Hanns took bearings on shoreside landmarks with the compass binoculars and went down below to plot them on the chart." Can you alter course about five degrees to starboard? We're coming in a bit south."

Carla smiled at him over the bridge deck and hit the correction button on the autopilot.

Hanns stood up and looked aft through the companionway. The *Seventh Chakra's* wake curved off to his left.

Saturday traffic increased as they approached the inlet. Sport fishing boats blasted by, heading home with their day's catch while dozens of smaller sail and power vessels converged on the channel.

The sun fell slowly, silhouetting the coastline ahead, fading gradually from yellow to orange to red.

"See the channel, Carla? The inlet's got tall condo buildings on the north side and houses on the other. Everything's well-marked but we want to make sure we clear the jetty that extends out on the south side."

"Yep. . .I have the markers in sight."

"Can you make out the tower on Peanut Island inside the channel?"

"Yes, and the old Coast Guard station with the red roof. We've got an easy shot here."

Hanns climbed over the bridge deck into the cockpit. "Funny; I'm used to navigating shallow, unmarked cuts in the Bahamas. When I get back to the States where all the channels are dredged and lit up, I still make landfall like it's some sort of adventure. These kids in their weekend waterski boats rocket in and out like they own the place. Here I am plotting my course on the chart."

Carla giggled. "They take the joy out of boating by making it easy here. This will be our last taste of Bahamian adventure for a while. Navigating is part of the fun—makes me feel like a real sailor."

"Well, my dear, if I seem a bit nervous, navigating isn't my worry. When I left Florida a year ago, I had just lost Raquel and the *Seventh Chakra* wasn't finished. I wanted out of the U.S. so I split without clearing out through Customs. As far as I know, I'm listed as an illegal alien who overstayed his visa and never left the country."

Carla squeezed his hand. "I don't imagine you have much to worry about. It'll be easy enough to document that we've been together in the Bahamas this past year. My own passport's in order. Play dumb about checking out if you're questioned. If you'd been here without a visa, they might give you a hard time, but did you get your passport stamped in Nassau when you sailed from Florida to the Bahamas?"

"Sure."

"Well, that'll prove you're not an illegal alien. I can't imagine you'll get more than a mild hassle over creating paperwork for some poor schmuck in an office somewhere."

"You're probably right."

"Probably," she smiled. "Once in a while."

"So let's get ready to make our right turn. Right inside, in front of Peanut Island, there's an anchoring area." Hanns pulled the chart up into the cockpit and pointed out the tiny anchor symbol. "When you get in, don't go too far inside; the anchorage shoals up in back. Just angle in and put her right about *here.* Ready?"

Hanns walked forward and pulled the quick-release pin on the anchor. He pointed to starboard and Carla aimed the *Seventh Chakra's* bow into the anchorage. Hanns signaled her to slow down but continue moving forward at near-idle speed. She shifted into neutral, letting the sloop's weight carry her to a stop. Hanns dropped the anchor and let the chain pay out as Carla engaged the engine in reverse. He snubbed up the line on a foredeck cleat and heard it creak under the strain as the anchor caught in the muddy bottom. At his signal, she pulled the fuel shutoff on the diesel, anticipating the peaceful quiet that follows a long motor trip.

"Quite a show over by the inlet, eh?" noted Hanns. *The Seventh Chakra* rested at anchor in the middle of several dozen other anchored boats, her bow facing the channel. Hanns stood on the foredeck gesturing over the rail to where police boats with flashing blue lights, helicopters and a white Coast Guard cutter streamed out of the inlet.

"Yeah. What do you think's going on?"

"The commotion is probably unrelated to us, but you know that radar reflector mounted up by the mast spreaders?"

"That silver, sort of spherical metal thingy?"

"Exactly. I tried out a bunch of different radar reflectors because when you're out at sea at night, you want to look like a big ship to the radar of a freighter. I've seen this reflector on other boats' radars. You can easily pick the *Seventh Chakra* out of a crowded anchorage; this thing lights up like a supernova. I wonder if they thought a big ship was moving into the channel? We tucked in behind these buildings and the signal disappeared. Nobody called for a harbor pilot. Then *boom;* we're gone. Did the ship sink? What happened?"

"No idea, but two helicopters are cruising back and forth and I see a Coast Guard launch. I counted at least four police boats."

"Carla, I have no idea what's going on. I can't think of any reason I'd be in trouble, but this scene gives me an uncomfortable vibe. Help me get the mainsail cover on. I want to lie here in this anchorage like we've been sitting among these other boats for weeks, minding our own business. If someone comes by asking questions, they can search the boat for all I care but the less we look like we just got here, the better."

He grabbed the sail cover out of the starboard cockpit locker. Carla helped with snaps and zippers.

Twenty minutes later, the police boats made their way back inside Palm Beach Inlet and dispersed into the Intracoastal Waterway. A helicopter zoomed low over the anchorage before moving on.

"If it's all the same to you, I'm going to indulge my paranoia and skip clearing in."

"Hanns, I'm with you whatever you decide to do. Sleep on it. I've sailed with you long enough to trust your instincts. If something's not right, I'd sure like to know what but I'm okay with forgetting to clear Customs."

"I appreciate the support. Let's make some dinner, wait for the cops to find something else to keep them busy, and put the dinghy in the water. Back when I first launched the *Seventh Chakra,* my neighbor in the next slip was a guy named Fred Smith. I did some work on his boat and he told me he was building a house out in LaBelle, Florida. He offered me a dock space any time. LaBelle is not exactly next door to Palm Beach, but it's less than two hours away by car and free dockage makes a hell of a difference."

"Where's LaBelle?"

"The St. Lucie Canal runs from Stuart, Florida to Lake Okeechobee across the middle of the state. Another canal on the other side of the lake goes through to the west coast of Florida. LaBelle is about a third of the way down the far canal. Ready for a little adventure on the inland waterways? Inland boating is mostly motoring, but it should be an interesting trip."

"How far from here to Stuart? Is there an inlet or do we stay inside and go up the waterway?"

"Tomorrow, we'll jump back out, head north about thirty-five miles and come back in at Stuart. We'll motor another ten or twelve miles to the St. Lucie canal and then the trip to Lake Okeechobee is a little less than thirty miles. Once we're inland, everything's farms, pastures, cows, bible thumpers, seasonal snowbirds and rednecks; God's country."

"Hallelujah! Another adventure. I'm in no hurry. Let's go."

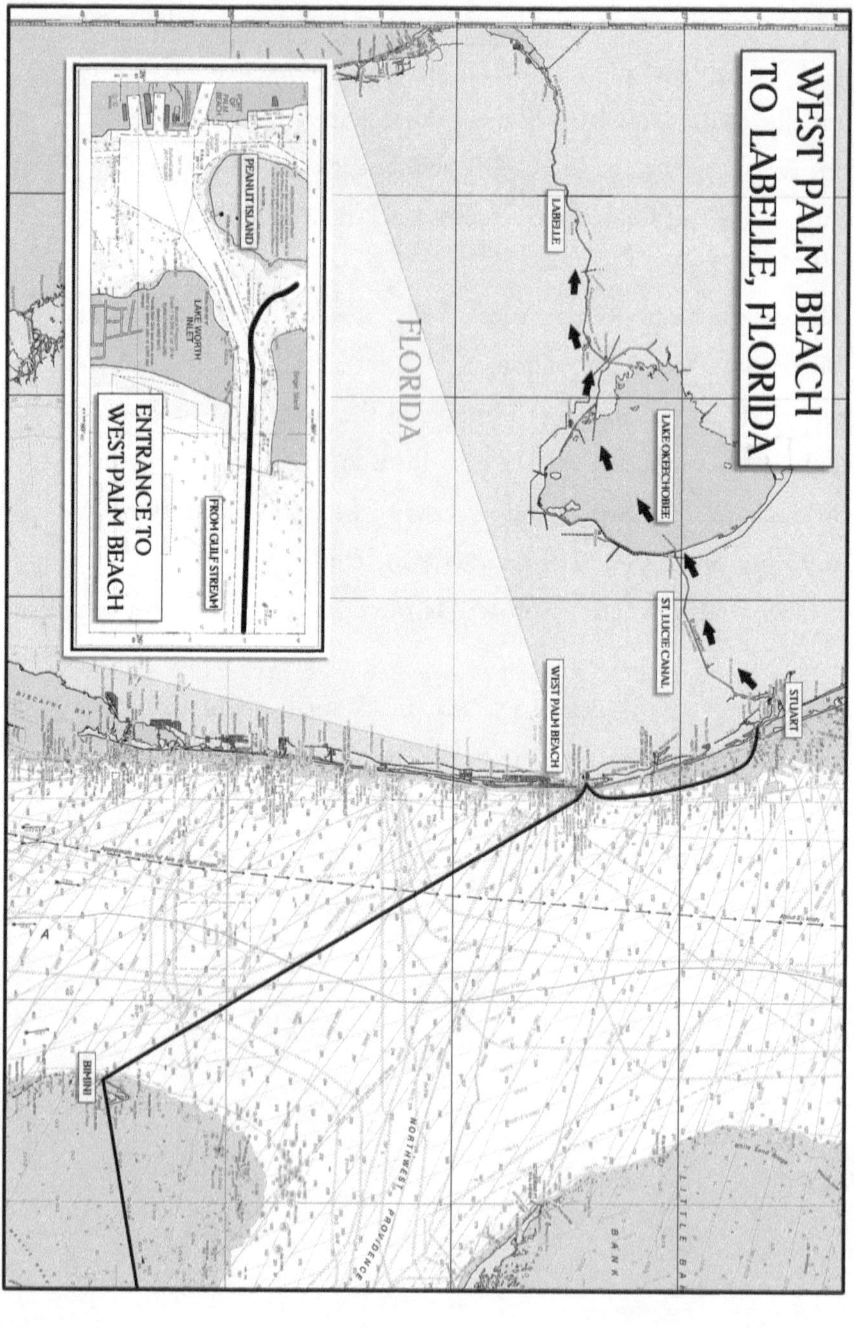

WEST PALM BEACH TO LABELLE, FLORIDA

LABELLE

LAKE OKEECHOBEE

ST. LUCIE CANAL

STUART

WEST PALM BEACH

FLORIDA

PEANUT ISLAND

LAKE WORTH INLET

FROM GULF STREAM

ENTRANCE TO WEST PALM BEACH

BIMINI

NORTHWEST PROVIDENCE

BANK

The St. Lucie Canal

"*The Seventh Chakra* glided over the dark waters of the St. Lucie Canal through farms, cow pastures, fields of sugar cane and swamps. An otter played at the water's edge. Hanns snapped a photograph as his ship ghosted by. The climate was hot and almost windless; the shade of the cockpit awning offered little relief.

After so many years at sea, Hanns found something amusing about driving his boat across the land like an automobile. All sailors experience 'the dream,' the one where they're driving their boat down the street of their town or neighborhood. The dream reflects a certain sense of not fitting in, of having been changed by one's experiences traveling across the water, which, itself, is symbolic of consciousness. Returning to civilization after a long absence makes one wonder if it's possible, or even desirable, to shed one's 'wilderness clothes.' Today, in the waking world, the sloop followed an endless line of utility poles and power lines across a landscape dressed in drab greens instead of sparkling blues.

At the end of the first day of inland cruising, in a small pond cut out of the canal's north edge just east of the bridge at Indiantown. Hanns dropped anchor. Thundersqualls spawned by heat rising from the flat, wet Everglades wandered across the western horizon like nuclear mushroom clouds. Rushing sounds of cars issued occasionally from the nearby span but the silence was filled not by waves lapping against the hull, but by a chorus of frogs, insects and land creatures whose nocturnal music was not typically heard through the open hatches of a cruising yacht.

Protected by mosquito screens he'd had the foresight to install before dark, Hanns lay under the fan in the main saloon on one of the two large settees. "Tomorrow, we'll get through the lock. If we're lucky, we'll get some wind to push us across Lake Okeechobee. Hopefully we'll even get some sails up?"

"Amen, Hanns. This trip is interesting but the sound of the motor gets old. The rattling masks many of life's subtler details."

In the morning, Hanns let Carla sleep while he pulled the anchor and got under weigh. Awakened by the engine, she joined him in the cockpit, smiled and kissed him. "I'll put breakfast together; I'm afraid we won't be dining on hogfish or lobster omelettes this morning."

"No problem. One of the joys of not clearing customs is nobody confiscates your Bahamian mangoes and papayas. The big yellow one in the food hammock is ripe and ready; it'll be delicious with a splash of lemon."

Carla went below to scrape the seeds from the orange flesh of the papaya. "Here in Florida, the Cubans don't call this 'papaya;' they call it *fruta bomba.* Papaya is slang for 'pussy.' I made the mistake once of going into a Cuban restaurant and ordering a glass of *jugo de papaya;* I brought the house down."

Hanns laughed. "If only the weather wasn't so damned hot, it wouldn't be a bad idea. Perhaps we could combine the two?"

"I should have known mentioning that would inspire your spirit of innovation. Why don't you enjoy some *fruta bomba* this morning, keep your eyes on the road and your hands on the tiller? Get me near some cool breeze and you can enjoy any kind you like."

Carla brought two wooden plates of the yellow-skinned fruit up into the cockpit. "This is a good, sweet one."

"Delicious!" Hanns sat on the bridge deck under the dodger,[20] avoiding the sun and steering with the tiller extension with his plate balanced in his lap.

"Definitely," offered Carla. "In spite of the heat, I'm enjoying this. I was sad Palm Beach was going to be the endpoint of our Bahamas cruise, but here we are, still voyaging off into the unknown together."

"Ain't dis de life deluxe?"

"Amen...and I think we're coming into Port Mayaca. The crazy bridge is just up ahead."

"Looks like a rusty clock mechanism," observed Hanns, "with those two big pulleys at the top."

20 A *dodger,* usually made of canvas on a metal frame, serves as a windshield for the front of the cockpit, protecting the occupants from spray and sun.

"The guide book says Port Mayaca is the lowest bridge on the cross-Florida canal system—a nuisance for sailors. At high water, which it happens to be, the clearance is 49 feet. Apparently, you can hire a local service to put big water jugs on your side deck. They fill them up with a pump to heel your boat over so the mast won't stick up so high."

"I once had a girlfriend who loved scraping details out of the cruising guide—one of her more redeeming features unfortunately—but as far as the Port Mayaca bridge goes, we should be able to slip underneath. We're a few inches over 45 feet high. Then, the distance from the bridge to the lock is a little under a mile. Once we hit Okeechobee, we'll enjoy thirty miles of open water."

Hanns gazed up at the rusty brown span as they passed beneath a section of railroad track hoisted overhead to allow them through. They continued on toward the lock. A short while later, they entered an open gate and tied up behind *Kicking Bass,* a nondescript, beige, fiberglass power boat apparently drawn up by someone accustomed to designing refrigerators and shipping containers. Carla glanced up at Hanns and smiled, anticipating his response to the vessel's lack of graceful line.

A bell rang. The lock door closed slowly behind them. "Carla, take the bow line. Take up the slack as the water comes in." I'll stand aft near the cockpit and manage the stern line. A moment later, the doors on the lake side opened a few inches. The lock began to flood. What had been a fifteen foot high seawall was soon barely higher than the *Seventh Chakra's* deck. As they rose with the water, a few spare, white administrative buildings and a small parking lot revealed themselves. When the water level inside the lock reached the level of the lake beyond it, another bell rang and the doors swung open. Hanns signaled Carla to let go of the bow line. They continued through the gate into the open waters of Lake Okeechobee.

"Quite a system, that lock."

Hanns explained, "when you connect the fresh water Everglades to the ocean with canals, you risk introducing saltwater into a delicate fresh water ecosystem. In this case, the freshwater ecosystem in question contains all the drinking water for the State of Florida, plus there's a dike built around the lake so it can hold more water than nature designed it to. Without those locks, you'd never get the lake water any higher than high tide and over time, you'd utterly wreck the environment. It's quite convenient to be able to run a boat across, rather than around, a peninsula the size of Florida but placing a few mechanical gates between the saltwater and ecological catastrophe borders on hubris."

Carla closed her eyes and smiled. "I suppose, my dear, but on a lighter note, I detect a bit of breeze and the feel of open water.

Let's haul up some sails and let the auto-pilot do the busy work; this may be our last chance to sail for a while."

"An excellent idea."

Late in the afternoon, Hanns spotted channel markers leading through the low marshland off Clewiston at the southwestern end of the lake. He switched on the engine once again, rolled up the furling jib[21] and after taking down the mainsail, stacked the canvas neatly on the boom. As they entered the marshes, he pointed to a large alligator floating at the edge of the channel. "We's in Flahridah, nayao," announced Hanns in his best hillbilly accent.

"Sugar cane country; see the fires off to the northwest?" Carla pointed to rising clouds of black smoke on the horizon. "They cut the cane down and then burn off all the leaves and undesirable parts of the plant. Every once in a while, we get a northwest wind; everything in Palm Beach gets covered with soot."

"I experienced a soot storm in the Abacos once, in the northern Bahamas. Probably, the soot came from here. Fortunately for the Bahamas, westerly winds rarely hang around long at this latitude.

"Anyway, here's our right turn. We'll follow the perimeter of the lake northwest for ten more miles and then stop at Moore Haven. Maybe we can find a place to eat, grab some supplies and get off

---

21 Instead of lowering, unclipping and bagging the sail as one does with a traditional jib, a line is pulled that rotates a *furling* drum at the base of the sail, causing the sail to roll up on the stay like a window shade.

the boat for a few hours? I'll call Fred Smith; we should be able to get to his place by lunchtime tomorrow. LaBelle is only about twenty five miles from Moore Haven."

"Sounds like a plan. I can handle being stuck on the boat, but being confined to an endless canal gets old."

"Not much farther to go. We'll pass through a lock at Moore Haven and another farther along at Ortona a bit more than halfway down the Caloosahatchee Canal. After that, the waterway connects to the sea; the canal opens up at Fort Meyers into the Gulf of Mexico on the other side of the state."

"Have you been here before, Hanns? I'm the one holding the guide book."

"No, this is my first time but the lights and sirens at Palm Beach Inlet have me thinking something's up. I've been going over the charts in detail and getting the lay of the land. I don't know if I'm being paranoid, but I'll feel better if I'm on top of things instead of taking the road one marker at a time."

The next morning, after Hanns's call for directions on the VHF, Fred Smith came down to the pier to welcome them and catch their dock lines. "Your timing is perfect. I'm leaving for the Bahamas in two or three days; the house is all yours. I'll get a kick out of knowing I'm hosting a celebrity but please, I don't like guns on the property." Fred smiled through his salt-and-pepper moustache, winking as if he was in on a private joke.

Hanns looked confused.

"You are Hanns Laldafia, right?"

"Yes."

"Don't you want to know how I know your full name? And by the way, I appreciate you being straight with me."

"I assume I told you my name, and I have nothing to hide. As for guns, I've got a .45 stashed on the boat but I've never fired it and I wasn't planning on arming myself. What's up?"

"Come on..." Fred put his hands on his hips. He stared at Hanns quizzically.

"Fred, I...I have no idea what..."

"You really don't, do you?"

"Fred, I'm drawing a complete blank...please enlighten me."

"They stick a magazine called *Scene* in the Sunday newspaper every week. The day after you phoned from Palm Beach, *Scene* featured an article about the Federal Marshals; Hanns Laldafia is one of the article's 'most wanted' fugitives. Apparently, you're wanted for 'gunrunning,' and you're in good company, too; yours is the last picture on the inside under the text; Josef Mengele is on the cover."

Carla raised an eyebrow.

Fred took a breath, looked down for a moment and then spoke directly. "Hanns, if all this is groundless bullshit, I'm behind you. Tie up here as long as you like, but you can surely understand why I had to ask. In a few days, I won't even be here—I have an alibi—but if I'm caught sheltering one of the most wanted men in America, the repercussions could be…"

"Fred, I'm looking you straight in the eye. I *promise* I have no idea what this is all about. I've been cruising for years and I'm one of the few people from that world who steadfastly avoided getting sucked into smuggling or any of those games. I passed up any number of opportunities to get involved with that sort of shit and I watched a lot of unfortunate people get into all sorts of stupid trouble.

"I've had my share of fun and mischief. I snuck up to the front row of life's theater many times and slipped into an empty seat, but I promise you this is some kind of bizarre joke. I can't think of a reason in the world…" Hanns paused. A distant memory of an encounter at a bar in St. Lucia flashed across his mind. *Sister Goldenhair Surprise.*

Fred and Carla looked at each other and then at Hanns.

Hanns took a slow, deep breath. "If you have a little time, I want to share a very interesting story with you."

The Tampa Gang

"The good news is if I had to find somewhere to disappear into the woodwork, this place is perfect, Fred. While I figure out what the hell is going on, I won't put you in any more jeopardy than I have to. If I can tie to your dock, renting someone a slip without doing a background check is hardly a crime.

"An old friend lives not far from here near Tampa. I hung out with Brother Willy back in Germany during the seventies; he was a neighbor of mine. He bailed out of the German Army and started a business importing English fashions, but he apparently had some sort of side business he never told me about. He called me one day to ask for a lift from the airport in Frankfurt. The terminal was an hour away, but sure, I was happy to help him out. On the way home, he asked if we could stop at his friend's place. The house was along the way so I said, 'no problem.' I dropped him off and he suddenly ran back out, jumped in the car and said, 'go!'

"The next morning, four cops were waiting at my house to question me about what I was doing with Willy. I told them the truth; I picked up my old neighbor from the airport and gave him a ride. Whatever bubble he'd been floating in had burst. He must have been under surveillance. I never asked what he was up to but he called me from Tampa a few weeks later, and I was good enough to pack up his house and ship his property to him without asking questions. I pretty much had to go through all his stuff in the process; I didn't find anything remotely suspicious or illegal. I'm sure Willy's got some sort of monkey business going on, but he's a slick operator. He'll know what's what and who's who as far as the cops, the rules and how to play the game. He owes me a favor and he's good for it in a sort of 'honor among thieves' kind of way.

"I'm not going to risk clearing in or out or running anywhere until I either fix this or let the coals die down. The Bahamas and the Gulf Stream are crawling with the U.S. Coast Guard, the DEA and the Junior G-Men these days. And all this 'zero tolerance' witch hunt bullshit won't work in my favor, especially offshore where nobody's paying attention to what the 'good guys' do."

Fred paused, then covered his mouth, his eyes and his ears in succession. "Just keep out of trouble. The house is yours if you..."

"Thanks, Fred, but we'll stay right here on the boat. I don't want to camp out in your house with this storm happening. We've already seen how this kind of shit can follow a person home. I won't risk contaminating your life with my problems. I'll visit Brother Willy and find out if he can help...or if I'll be jumping from the frying pan into the fire."

"I'll be home all day tomorrow working on the boat and getting ready to leave, Hanns. Take my car and go see your friend. For now, you can sleep inside the house or on the boat; I don't care. After I sail off, take the air-conditioner that's sitting in my boat's companionway. I won't bring the AC cruising with me and you'll need it while I'm gone; summers are mighty hot and humid here."

Morning arrived in an explosion of pastel pinks and oranges flooding through live oaks festooned with Spanish moss. Hanns stood under the pleasure dome peeking out the companionway over the bridge deck, studying the mangrove roots next to the dock while Carla got dressed and ready.

"Hanns, are you sure visiting this guy Willy is a good idea? After all, he sucked you into a potential minefield of..."

"Yeah, he did use me for cover, but he also knew I wasn't involved; I didn't know anything I wasn't supposed to. I can't say it was the nicest thing anyone's ever done for me but what happened? The cops questioned me and let me go. Willy didn't perpetrate any kind of malicious act.

"Back in Germany when we were neighbors in the same village, we used to practice martial arts together. Willy was the one who introduced me to kendo swords; we had a lot of good times. I visited him with Raquel back when we were in Florida looking for boats.

He's a respected business man in Tampa now. He has a big gravel company; they do landscaping, driveways, pool decks and the like. Willy's got a crew of hard workers and he works pretty hard himself.

"But as I think back, something else comes into focus. When I got to the U.S. with *Sorcery* back in the early seventies, I rented a slip in a marina behind a supermarket. The marina manager came down to the boat and told me a few people were waiting on the dock to speak to me. They flashed badges and asked what I was doing. I explained I was cruising through on my sailboat; 'Is there any problem?' They were polite enough, but they asked if they could take my picture—the same picture Fred showed us in the *Scene* magazine. After associating with Willy in Germany, did I get stuck on a blacklist of people to watch? I wonder if that's why Yvonne jumped on *Chaos* with me back in '76. Is this shit all connected…or am I getting paranoid trying to make sense of something that doesn't make sense?"

"Do you think this 'most wanted' thing is a twisted revenge trip for what happened when you split with Secret Agent Surprise in the Dominican Republic?" proposed Carla.

"Either that or possibly, when she jumped on board, she figured I was going to be some sort of big trophy bust. I turned out to be a nice guy trying to enjoy the islands and stay out of trouble. Maybe she needed to make me look like 'the big one that got away' so she could save face with her agency buddies? In the end, it turned out it was *me* who busted *her*.

"What kills me is all the people who simply refuse to believe the truth. I'm an honest guy who went to college, worked hard and paid my dues as a filmmaker. I put my savings in a sailboat and spent the past ten years odd-jobbing my way through paradise. I never got involved in theft, fraud, smuggling, violence, guns, real estate, government or greed, and all I ever asked of the world is to be allowed to go peacefully on my way. Instead, a fucking army of people is convinced that someone who lives the way I live must be hiding something or running an illegal business. To seek the truth is one thing. To deny it is another. To *invent* the truth and use that fabrication to create a purpose for the wheels of industry and government is a different thing altogether.

"People simply won't believe paradise has an open door. You aren't required to pray, become a monk, seek forgiveness, accept Jesus, walk on hot coals, send a tax-deductible check or feed a starving child to get in. You aren't required to live your life miserable so you can be happy after you die. All you have to do is let go of the entanglements you create for yourself, cut the cord and walk out into the beautiful world. The same realization hit you after we freed the dolphins that night in Nassau, Carla. Why else are you here with me now? What did it ultimately take to leave a ten-year job and lifestyle behind? A moment of inspiration and a phone call.

"The only crime I ever committed—beyond a few mischievous pranks I'm frankly proud of—is to force people who question me to confront their own choices. Most of the idiots who get in my way make ten times my income but they have one one-hundredth my quality of life. I'm not saying they're all unhappy but few of them imagine sailing the tropics is on their list of options. The gates of paradise are wide open but they're guarded by a gang of sad little people who want everyone to sit outside and save the good life for later. I can't appease them without being dishonest. I can't help if my lifestyle smashes their fragile little idols, but I'm sure tired of being profiled based on the way they expect people to behave in their tiny, shitty, little world."

Carla took a deep breath. "Speaking of tiny little worlds, I'm going to hold off on visiting my parents for a few days. I figure they can deal with their Jewish daughter's German boyfriend but if they get wind of this latest fiasco, I worry they'll try to 'do the right thing.' I don't want them making any phone calls inspired by parental protectiveness or a misdirected sense of civic duty."

"Sounds like a plan, my dear. Ready to hit the road?"

After an hour-and-a-half of driving, Hanns and Carla pulled through a chain link gate into a gravel driveway shaded by live oak trees. A collection of work vehicles mingled with a handful of shiny BMWs and Mercedes. A few hopped-up four-wheel-drive pickup trucks were pulled off the gravel onto the grass. A spot was left open for Hanns and Carla's borrowed Volkswagen Rabbit close to the door.

Hanns took Carla's hand, sauntered up to the porch and was about to knock when Brother Willy opened the door and announced loudly, "Boys, the guest of honor is here."

Hanns paused to let a few pit bull dogs sniff the back of his hand and then walked in to embrace Brother Willy. Willy was in his fifties, balding with a forked salt and pepper beard. Thick and broad-shouldered, he projected the essence of calm power. He surveyed Carla and took her fingers in his large, calloused hand. "Welcome. I told the boys who was coming; they insisted on being here to meet you. You're looking at over a century of collective jail time in this room but nobody's ever made the honor roll like you. There's a huge stack of *Scene* magazines here you'll have to sign before they let you out of here."

Hanns laughed out loud. "Sorry to disappoint you but the whole thing is either a bad practical joke or a big mistake. I'm clueless about how I ended up on the magazine. I never…"

"Aw, who do you think you're fuckin' with, Doc? We all have our secrets here; nobody's asking or telling. We understand, but you 'got yer picture on the cover of the Rollin' Stone;' you're a celebrity.

Willy clapped him on the back with a clubby arm. All Hanns could do was shrug at Carla as he ushered them into the room.

"Hanns, you're a hero here. Anything you want, we'll set you up. Need a fake ID? A car? Money? Dope? A girlfriend?" Willy paused for a moment and looked at Carla. "Sorry, but we want to make sure our man is covered. You can both hide out here as long as you want. We're livin' the good life. You're among friends. You want something, just ask."

A big tattoo-covered man raised his beer can. "Anyone fucks with you, let us know; we'll take 'em out." A chorus of approving shouts followed from around the room.

"Blackjack went out into the bush a few days ago and killed a wild pig with his hunting knife. We lit up a barbecue out back that'll blow your fucking mind. You guys come out, kick back and take a load off. You'll meet everyone soon enough; nobody's shy around here. Whatcha drinking, Doc?"

"Gunrunnin' huh?" A wiry man with a KILL 'EM ALL. LET GOD SORT 'EM OUT t-shirt took Hanns's hand. "I'm A.J. If you like guns, I got a collection of custom shotguns you jes' gotta see. My daddy got his daddy's collection and I been continuin' the family tradition. I gots a whole room in my freakin' house full o' nothin' but firearms.

"Here, check this out." A.J. pulled out a gold-plated .357 magnum revolver covered with filigree engraving. "Them handles is made from a piece o' crystallized fuckin' meteorite. Them crisscross patterns form when melted iron out in space cools 'bout 1 degree every million years; goddamnedest shit I ever come across."

Hanns accepted the firearm and admired the machine work. He opened the cylinder and inspected the mechanism, pretending an affinity for firearms. He pulled back the hammer with his thumb to feel the tension before handing the weapon back. "This piece has never been fired, has it?"

"No, but I ain't sentimental 'bout shit like that. I ain't 'zackly runnin' 'round *lookin'* to pull the trigger, but the first sonofabitch who crosses me's gonna get killed by a piece o' goddamned art. Now *that's* funny. Good to finally meet you, Doc. Willy's told us all 'bout you, 'n' we've been lookin' forward to you joinin' us. Welcome to the goddamned family."

A.J. walked off toward the barbecue grill studying his revolver and laughing.

Brother Willy came over and put a hand on Hanns's shoulder. "Don't worry about my lunatic fringe. Some of these boys spent a little too much time burning villages in Vietnam thinking they were killing communists for Uncle Sam. They came home and got their first speeding ticket; it blew their minds. A few others are poor weeds that sprouted in bad soil. They're a rough bunch; most of them aren't very well-educated, but they're loyal and hard-working. They have a home here with people who care and understand. We work hard at the gravel business during the day. At night and on weekends, we run an import business that earns substantially more..."

Hanns waved his hand. "The gravel business is all I need to know about. I'm not afraid of hard work in the sun if you can give me a job, and I'm a good engineer. Maybe I can help with some of the planning and design as far as making sure your installations happen with finesse?"

"We all make pretty handsome money. If you want, you can…"

"No. Thanks. Just a job in the gravel business. No fake IDs. No cover-ups. I'm going to accept and appreciate your help with lying low for a while but hiding is not my nature. There's a difference between quietly minding your own business and running away. I'm going to buy a car and register it in my own name. I'll get my own bank account and a phone."

"But, Hanns…"

"No, Willy. As soon as I start acting like a fugitive, I'll be one. I've been a free sailor for ten years now and I'm not about to go on the defensive because a bunch of idiots entered my face in a poster competition. If they come for me, whatever happens will happen, but my conscience is clean. What I suspect will happen is absolutely nothing. The people who set me up are small-minded bureaucrats who use their professional influence to advance their personal agendas. They're the ones who should be running and covering their tracks; I don't think they want their game unraveling on top of them. I survived all sorts of shit in my life. As far as I'm concerned, this incident is a fart in a hurricane. I'm going to live my life, work a legitimate job, enjoy some time living ashore and give these assholes all the clues they need to knock on my door. Nothing will happen. The Marshals; the FBI; the Alcohol, Tobacco and Firearms People; the DEA—do you think any of them talk to each other? They're in the trophy-hunting business; they all want to stalk their own game. At the same time, none of these guys wants to get duped into shooting a stuffed buck. Let them do their homework; they'll find easier people to prosecute and better reasons to go after them. So what if I'm on a list? This planet is my home; I'm going to go where I want and live how I want."

"You've got some balls, man, but sure. I have an old Volkswagen Beetle—good German hardware—it's yours if you can get the engine running. If you want anything else—anything at all—let me know."

"A job, the Beetle and a place to bunk down when I'm working up here a hundred miles from my boat would be manna from heaven... but yes...there is just one more thing."

"Name it, Doc."

"I noticed a red Ferrari parked out front. I went road-tripping in a Lamborghini Miura once upon a time. I know how to handle a big-horsepower machine and I'd love to show Carla what it's like to ride in a real sports car."

"I'll go get the keys from Wilson. That's an easy one."

Speed

"Hop in. How does she feel?"

Carla lowered herself into the bucket seat, holding tight to a leather strap hanging from the overhead. "Hmmm...deep?"

"Exactly. These machines are all about low center of gravity; your ass is six inches off the asphalt. Hang a tight turn going ninety and this baby'll grab the road like she's on rails. The bucket seats keep you from flying out the window. We're pilots for a high performance engine. Sailing is infrared; racing cars are ultraviolet—extreme but opposite frequency ranges beyond the spectrum of ordinary, visible fun." Hanns turned the key and revved the motor, getting a sense for the throttle response. "Familiarize yourself with this map. You're the official navigator."

"Me?"

"A few miles north of here, we'll find nothing but long, straight roads through orange groves. They all look the same, especially at night. We're about to drive on those roads at three times the legal speed limit."

"Hanns, are you sure this is a good idea?"

"I'm sure it's *not;* that's part of the fun."

The Ferrari rumbled through Brother Willy's open gate and headed north toward I-4.

"How fast are we going?"

"Right now we're barely idling but you're a lot closer to the road than you're used to; you'll think you're going faster than we actually are. I don't want to create any disturbance around Willy's place so I'll wait until we're on highway 41; there's a stretch where the road wraps around a big piece of swampland. Better to go flying where there's less chance of an orange truck puttering out in front of us without looking."

"Kind of a rough bunch back at Willy's, don't you think?"

"Nut cases every one of them, but they're convinced I'm some sort of master criminal. I'm not getting involved in their side business so they're giving me the perfect cover. With a job on the gravel crew, I can earn enough money to make upgrades to the *Seventh Chakra.* I figure I'll do that for six months or so. Afterward, we can go down to the Caribbean before hurricane season starts—or given the sphincter factor there, maybe we should think about the Mediterranean? In the meantime, I'll try to figure out what this *Scene Magazine* crap is about and if I can't, then fuck it. I'm going to enjoy my fun until someone tries to prosecute me. For all I know, the whole thing's a big practical joke but I won't let it ruin my life."

"Hanns, Willy dug his own rattlesnake pit to practice kendo swords in. That guy they call 'Blackjack' killed a wild boar with a hunting knife. I've never seen so many guns, tattoos, confederate flags and swastikas in one place. I'm a 'nice Jewish girl;' I hate to tell you: those people don't exactly give me a 'peaceful, easy feeling.'"

"As a nice German boy, I confess I totally agree but as much as they're profoundly ignorant in certain ways, they keep their own code of honor; they're not going to turn me in or turn me out. I've known Willy since the late sixties; I can assure you he's no more a Nazi than I am but he gets a certain status among his band of pirates by virtue of his being German. Those guys don't know *anything* about what happened in Germany. They view the whole Nazi thing as a massive antiestablishment celebration. The S.S. had their skull-and-crossbones schtick happening; that offers the same adolescent appeal as the Harley Davidson ethos if you don't have the education to connect the *reich* to some of the greatest atrocities in human history. In a gang like theirs, I suspect each member poses as a caricature of himself for the others—and ultimately for himself—like a band of kids who try to impress each other by acting tough. In this case, the kids never grew up, but with the amount of dope they're smoking, I doubt they fight anyone, lynch anyone or even genuinely hate anyone. Their fantasy world makes for entertaining tough talk over beer and football when the bass aren't running and there aren't any busty women around, but if you don't back one of these guys into a corner and force him to prove himself in front of his friends, all you've got left to deal with is a redneck who talks trash because it's all he knows how to talk about. If I thought these boneheads were genuine white supremacist, Nazi confederates, I'd head in a different direction but they're just another slice of the American pie.

"I don't know what Willy's side business is but knowing his history, it's probably dope-related. We're driving a borrowed Ferrari—which suggests they bring in a sizable amount of cash—but laundering that kind of money means working your ass off. These guys are wealthy but they toil all day in the Florida sun pouring and raking gravel to maintain the appearance they actually *earn* their money. Ironic: when you're on that train, at some point, you end up looking out the window and wondering if you're actually getting anywhere or if there's any place to get off.

"I'm an eternal optimist. What keeps me going is a certain hope that the games people play with each other and with themselves are naïve expressions of a young humanity. You can look at Brother Willy's lunatic fringe and conclude *homo sapiens* is not God's finest piece of work, but we're all born children; we all have to grow up. Not all of us do—and I don't believe you can change anyone who isn't ready and willing to change—but I'll be working and living alongside these guys without compromising my own values or lifestyle. I'm not going to pose as a Nazi or a bigot; I'm not going to actively try to influence anyone; but I'm an outsider who could be a catalyst for some kind of change or evolution. Maybe I'm being idealistic or even egotistical, but to me, this scenario makes a colorful experiment.

"Carla, you and I live in a world of culture, technology, education and philosophy, but one in five people in America reads at or below a fifth-grade level. You may think the kids we went to school with or the employees you worked with at the Department of Energy or the clients who hired me to produce documentary films are 'mainstream,' but all over the world, ignorant people hold insupportable beliefs. They make war with people they think are enemies, mix their religion into their governments and stand armed and ready to defend their points of view. We've been living in a comfortable world of smart, self-reliant sailors who work, read and travel. Why not take a few months off and experience the good, the bad and the ugly of an authentic slice of America? Think of this as an anthropology class."

"I see where you're coming from, Hanns, but the relationship between ignorance, fear and hatred makes me nervous. I don't want you to find yourself in a situation where you're forced to prove you're 'one of us' or 'one of them.'"

"Fair enough; I'm with you. This experiment has a short lifespan but I'm intrigued. I'll try this out. If the scene gets ugly or the vibe changes, I'll be back on the water the same day. I'm happiest on my boat, anyway.

"But while we're here on shore sorting things out and taking care of business, let's enjoy some adventure. Here's the stretch I pointed out on the map; hang on." Hanns downshifted and stepped on the gas. The Ferrari screamed and accelerated. Hanns shifted back up. "One-thirty, one-forty, one-fifty. Come on, baby, give me one sixty...come on."

Carla gripped the sides of her seat.

"One-sixty! I think that's all she's got."

"Oh, we've got more than one-sixty, Mister. We've got flashing blue lights left in the dust way behind us. I think he was hiding behind a billboard."

"I'll bet his radar gun blew up in his hand."

"What are you going to do?"

"I'm going to run like hell. You can bet he's already calling for his buddies in the next town to head this way. I'll switch off the lights and pull off onto one of these side roads. Got the map handy?"

"Yeah, but..."

"Carla, I just got tagged doing a hundred-sixty miles per hour. I'm not legally here in this country. I don't have insurance or a driver's license. I'm in a borrowed car I'm not carrying papers for, and for reasons beyond my power to imagine, I'm one of the most wanted men in the United States. What difference will it make if they have to chase me to catch me? If I get busted, I'll cop a plea and get the judge to drop the speeding charges."

"Good points. Make a left. Let the first cop pass behind us on the main road. Then, make another left on Mill Road; it's curvy and it crosses the railroad tracks so don't blow through too fast."

"Carla, open your window. These guys have their sirens blaring and their lights flashing; they're broadcasting their positions. We've got two, maybe three, cars on us now. With our windows down, we'll get more air than we'd like, but we'll hear where they are. If they had any brains, they'd be more stealthy."

Hanns pulled behind a closed fruit stand and waited for one of the police cars to fly by. "Good. Now back the way we came. They're checking the small access roads; I'll be safer on the main drag. They won't expect me to be that brassy, though they'd probably call me stupid. Look across that field. See the blue lights reflecting on the telephone poles?" Hanns doubled back to the main road, switched the lights back on and followed a line of a half-dozen cars up the on-ramp to the interstate.

A half hour later, Hanns pulled through Willy's gate where he was directed to park the Ferrari in the back yard.

Willy smiled. "The boys enjoyed your show on the police scanner. Wilson's always been too chickenshit to get that car up over ninety miles an hour. I'm guessing you topped her out? They're giving him a hell of a time about it. They clocked you going one fifty-seven and boy did they bitch when you turned your lights out!"

"What about Wilson. Is he going to…?"

A.J. helped Carla out the passenger door. "Ain't no big deal. They'll come 'round askin' 'im about his Ferrari; ain't too many folks 'round here who has one 'cept him. He'll tell 'em he was at a party, passed out and someone took his toy joy ridin'. Long's they didn't catch you, ain't much they can do.

"C'mon in and have a cold one," smiled Blackjack. "Ain't no worries here."

The Game

Hanns pushed Fred's silver Volkswagen Rabbit south through the night toward LaBelle. "I'll tell you; driving this thing is pretty boring after driving the Ferrari. I haven't had a chance to get behind the wheel of a high performance machine like that for many years. What a rush!"

"Hanns, can we talk? I can't wrap my head around the *Scene Magazine*, and the flea circus over at Brother Willy's is..."

"Carla, my dear, I've decided I'm just not going to worry about it."

"What do you mean 'you're not going to worry?' You were worried enough when you first found out. Why not get in touch with the person who wrote the *Scene* article? We can hire someone not obviously connected to us make some public records requests. A private investigator could easily put their hands on..."

"I was definitely taken by surprise when Fred confronted me with the article. Suddenly discovering you're one of America's most-wanted criminals is disconcerting. Am I curious to find out who's behind this? Sure, but think the matter through.

"First off, I never did anything wrong. Even if I somehow managed to *accidentally* do something illegal, I was certainly never involved in 'gunrunning,' and no way in hell did I *ever* do *anything* to earn myself the same criminal status as a butcher like Josef Mengele. Someone is playing a game here—an ugly, dishonest game—and they're obviously unconcerned about their own integrity or professionalism. I expect they'd show an equal disregard for whatever right to due process a German national might be entitled to here in the U.S.—and probably an equal disregard for my life."

"But you can say the same thing about Brother Willy and the Tampa Gang, too. Those guys are…"

"Those guys are *what?* Do you honestly think they're worse than the U.S. government who put a secret agent on my boat and endangered my life using me to host their spy base? I can't prove this situation is related to that but nothing else makes any sense. Is a band of rednecks with hunting knives and handguns any less sane or honest than the assholes who framed me for crimes I never committed? Whatever Willy's gang is up to won't come out of the closet in the middle of the night and kill you in your sleep. I won't offer them as the world's finest example of upright citizenship, but what you see is what you get. They practice a certain integrity I can't find in the government parasite who pretended to be my lover, my partner and my friend as part of her undercover job and who now, five years later, is still trying to track me down and make my life miserable. That's not criminal; that's pathological. We're talking some twisted shit here. Give me Brother Willy's lunatic fringe any day."

"But Hanns, I'm scared and concerned. I want to get behind you and help. You're not guilty of anything; we need to clear your name so we can go on living life together without sneaking around or looking over our shoulders."

"You know what I'm guilty of, Carla? I'm guilty of catching these bastards at their own game. They were playing me; they probably made a lot of plans based on me being their personal sucker. I got their number, gave them a spanking, walked out on them and those plans fell apart. Now, they expect me to hide or run or quake in fear. They're pissed off they can't catch up with me to 'teach me a lesson.'

"Examine the scenario from Sister Goldenhair's perspective. You traded your own traditional career for a life of freedom and adventure; I showed Yvonne the good life and she gave it up for her job. Maybe she wants to blame that on me but she was the one trying to live in two worlds; she was the one who cast herself out of Paradise.

"I'm also guilty of declaring the emperor is naked. I never accepted the rules at face value. I never bought into phony things like status or the idea you should work your entire life to keep up with the treadmill so you can enjoy a few years of retirement when you're old and creaky before your children throw you into a nursing home. I'm a man of limited means but I live a life most millionaires would envy. I'm free and that upsets people; they're way too invested in their own paths to accept cheaper, healthier, freer alternatives. I don't live the way I do to rub anyone's nose in my choices but some people see me as a threat to their world view; some of them feel threatened enough to come after me.

"Do you know what their game is now? Another lie; a smoke screen to flush me out of hiding. Don't you think they're waiting for someone to make a public records request or start an investigation? This is a trap set by sick people who would rather sit in the center of a web waiting to pounce on me than go live lives of their own. Do you think if they catch me, I'll get my day in court and a chance to clear my name? Don't be naïve. These are dangerous people with serious mental health problems and too much power.

"My plan is to leave the games to the players. If you play with cheaters, you lose but not playing at all is as good as winning. I'm not going to expose my whereabouts by acting guilty. I'm not hiding. I'm not running. Why should I? My mission is the same as before; to live life like I've got one day left."

"But what if they do catch up with you? What will you do?"

"I don't know. If they catch me, they catch me, but life's too short to worry about stupid shit. I raced cars in Europe and somehow managed to keep the tires on the road when there was no mathematical explanation for not spinning off the track and rolling over. I survived a battle in the desert in Saudi Arabia. I survived a highjacking and a terrorist ambush at a hotel in Jordan. I survived storms at sea. I sailed into the middle of coral reefs that should have killed me ten times over. I landed in Puerto Rico with Raquel and got detained by customs for having a phony rap sheet two pages long. Sound familiar? Any connection? What happened? A friend I didn't even know had any authority magically appeared to vouch for me. I walked out with a smile on my face. You and I freed the dolphins in Nassau, got away clean and started a life together. We came into Palm Beach thirty seconds ahead of half the law enforcement in Florida and then sat at Peanut Island Anchorage enjoying the show. Fred was here to offer us a boat slip for nothing. Willy offered me a car and a job. We just beat the police in a borrowed Ferrari and we're putt-putting home as happy as can be. I'm having an outrageous good time and I'm not going to let the Keystone cops slap a magnet on the side of my fun compass. Do you think it makes sense to hide, run away or invite some sort of confrontation with people who don't fight fair?

"The less I have to do with any of this bullshit, the happier and safer I'll be. If you haven't figured it out, I'm doing fine without engaging with these psychotic wackos and their criminal games. I want absolutely nothing to do with them. Let this be their game, not mine."

"Well, I'd be the last one to argue you don't have a charmed life, but I do think you should at least take it easy driving through these little towns. Florida's famous for speed traps."

"Now that I'll take as good advice." Hanns eased up on the gas and let the car coast to slow it down. "There's no reason to tempt fate. We're not in any hurry. Fred's place is just another mile or two down the road."

Blue lights flashed. A short note rose and decrescendoed on a police siren behind them.

Hanns pulled off onto the side of the highway and rolled down his window. Carla put her head in her hands. She looked down, defeated.

A Florida State Trooper slowly got out of his car, put on his cowboy hat, swaggered alongside and pointed his flashlight down into the Volkswagen. "Sir, do you know why I pulled you over?"

"I'm guessing I was going a little too fast, sir?"

"You're *guessing* you were going too fast or you *were* going too fast?"

"I'm sorry, officer. My friend here had just pointed out I was hotfooting it. I started to slow down, but...I won't waste your time with excuses or arguments. Yes, I was going faster than the speed limit; you caught me."

"You were doing fifty three in a forty-mile-per-hour zone. Can you show me your driver's license and registration please, sir?"

Hanns reached for his pocket, then patted his pants as if surprised to find it empty. "Oh, no. Sweetie, I must have left my wallet at the house. This is terrible timing. Officer, look...I..."

"Driving without a license? Is this your car?"

"The car belongs to a friend of mine; Fred Smith. He owns a house in LaBelle. You'll find it's registered in his name if you check the license plate. We can call him to verify he loaned it to me or just follow me back there. His home is only a mile from here and…"

"What's your name, sir?"

"Hanns. Hanns Laldafia."

"And your birthday?"

"July 13, 1948. Look, officer, I'm really sorry I don't have my papers with me. If you want, I can…"

The officer looked at Carla. "Ma'am, do you have a valid driver's license with you?"

"Yes sir, I do." Carla handed him her license.

The officer smiled as if he'd perpetrated a clever joke. "My birthday's also July 13, 1948. Why don't you two switch places for the ride home? Sir, please drive safely and carry your license with you next time. Enjoy your evening."

Postscript

Currents is a fictional account of true life events. The mystery of Werner's murder was never solved. Neither the nature of the charges against Hanns nor the identity of his antagonists was ever discovered. Hanns worked with the Tampa Gang for several months, before sailing south to Miami's Dinner Key Anchorage. Eventually, he cruised the *Seventh Chakra* across the Atlantic to Europe before returning to the Caribbean and ports beyond. He continues to live a life of adventure—one day at a time.

About the Author

Dave Bricker lives in Miami, Florida with his wife and daughter. He teaches graphic design and thesis writing at an Arts University. He lived aboard sailing yachts for fifteen years, cruising the Bahamas and the American East Coast, and sailing a wooden yawl across the Atlantic from the Bahamas to Gibraltar.

Currents is his third work of fiction. His first novels are *The Dance* and *Waves.* Dave Bricker is also the author of *The One-Hour Guide to Self-Publishing: Straight Talk For Fiction and Nonfiction Writers About Producing and Marketing Your Own Books.*

Blue Monk, a collection of stories from his own sailing experiences, will be published at the beginning of 2013.

Dave Bricker writes, designs and produces his own books, and publishes them through Essential Absurdities Press. For more information, please visit www.TheWorldsGreatestBook.com

Honoraria

Currents has benefited from the support of some extraordinary people. Ari, without your inspiring adventures and exceptional storytelling abilities, this book wouldn't exist at all. Thanks for being a friend these many years. Gregory Glass spent many hours reading, editing, revising, discussing and encouraging; your suggestions made an invaluable contribution. Thank you Richard Geller for sharing the publishing journey with me. Special thanks to Kim Aden for encouragement and editing, and to my friend and 'round-the-world sailor Neal Petersen for lots of tiny, technical details about multihull sailing. Al Gross, you're a fantastic proofreader; thanks for your discriminating eyes. Thanks to Jim Hesketh for reading and offering suggestions. Finally, thanks to Suzanne for many years of friendship and partnership, and to our amazing daughter Eva.

Colophon

The text of *Currents* is set in Centaur, a refinement of Roman inscriptional capitals designed by Bruce Rogers as a titling design for signage in the Metropolitan Museum. Rogers later designed a lowercase based on Nicolas Jenson's work from the mid-1460s, turning the titling into a full typeface.

The book's title and section headers are set in Raniscript, a contemporary typeface designed by Stephen Rapp. It adds a classic, decorative note reminiscent of Modernist book designs from the 1920s.

The corner ornament was selected from Lanston Typeface Corporation's Keystone Ornaments, a set of glyphs based on "running border" ornaments from the Keystone Type foundry of Philadelphia, circa 1903.

The titles on the chart illustrations and the Essential Absurdities Logotype are set in Behrens Antiqua, designed by Peter Behrens in 1902 as a corporate typeface to emulate hand-rendered display lettering while maintaining consistency across artists and applications. It was chosen for this book in homage to its creator and to a spirit of combining engineering with art that is characteristic of the real-life person upon whom this book's protagonist is based.

The book's margins are based on the Van de Graaf canon.

Author's Note

Currents was written, designed, produced and published by its author. Because independent writers and publishers should be held to the same high standards as the mainstream publishing industry, I encourage you to post an honest and objective review of this book in the online bookstore of your choice. Such dialogue only serves the cause of good writers and good readers.

Thank you,

Dave Bricker

www.ingramcontent.com/pod-product-compliance
Lightning Source LLC
Chambersburg PA
CBHW030426310726
48979CB00009B/1629/J

* 9 7 8 0 9 8 4 3 0 0 9 5 2 *